TALES OF
AMERICAN IDIOCY

TALES OF
AMERICAN IDIOCY

P.R.Infidel

LIBERTY HILL PUBLISHING

Liberty Hill Publishing
2301 Lucien Way #415
Maitland, FL 32751
407.339.4217
www.libertyhillpublishing.com

Paperback ISBN-13: 978-1-66286-073-7
Ebook ISBN-13: 978-1-66286-074-4

This book is dedicated to those who have been lost, wronged, and robbed in the early 2020s. May God avenge them.

Every time you make a choice you are turning the central part of you, the part of you that chooses, into something a little different than it was before. And taking your life as a whole, with all your innumerable choices, all your life long you are slowly turning this central thing into a heavenly creature or a hellish creature: either into a creature that is in harmony with God, and with other creatures, and with itself, or else into one that is in a state of war and hatred with God, and with its fellow creatures, and with itself. To be the one kind of creature is heaven: that is, it is joy and peace and knowledge and power. To be the other means madness, horror, *idiocy*, rage, impotence, and eternal loneliness. Each of us at each moment is progressing to the one state or the other.

—C. S. Lewis, *Mere Christianity*

PREFACE

America has entered an age of Idiocy—an age in which its citizens promote and practice self-destruction in exchange for a nebulous sense of security and self-righteousness. Worse, few Americans realize it.

It is with this sad and somewhat humorous reality in mind that I wrote this book. I hope that by reframing American Idiocy using the animal kingdom and the supernatural realm, I might help wake America from the mass formation psychosis in which she has found herself and lead her back to wisdom and freedom.

I hope you enjoy the following tales of American Idiocy.

REGARDING EVIL POLITICIANS AND IMMIGRATION WITHOUT REPRESENTATION

I regard it as completely unimportant who in the party will vote and how, but it is extremely important who will count the votes and how.

—Joseph Stalin

We Know What You Did Last Election

"We know what you did last election." The whisper filled his ears and then his mind, roaring above the band, the footsteps of the soldiers doing their pass and review, and the cries of the small, carefully selected crowd.

It was so loud, the voice, and so strange, that just-inaugurated President Joe Brandon couldn't tell if it was a roar or a whisper, human or alien, organic or echoing from a spiritual plane.

"We know what you did last election," the voice repeated, this time with the sing-song melody of a wind instrument, as though it had hitched a ride on the breeze from an orchestra. It was detached and ethereal, but clear and insistent. Someone had to have said it. But who?

Hadn't they removed anyone who had the remotest chance of even thinking such a thing?

President Brandon looked to his left at the sallow, frowning face of his wife. Her dyed blonde hair, brass as an antique bedpost, was ironically her most honest feature. It framed pale blue eyes, a sagging face, and a set of thin, frowning lips.

The frown seemed odd to the president. She should have been smiling, but she wasn't. She was wearing a mask of study and surmise bordering on fear.

Yes, Jane was afraid—afraid of what he might say or do next—but she hadn't spoken.

He looked to his left, but his vice president, Camille Harold, wasn't looking at him. She was standing straight, head forward, arms raised. She was fully focused on the cultivated crowd before them and, of course, on the cameras. She was terribly interested in performing for them.

No, Camille hadn't said that; Camille was too preoccupied with Camille.

The Secret Service had promised that they checked the social media and political leanings of all in attendance. Perhaps they hadn't, or they had, and . . .

President Brandon shook his head. No, it wasn't that. He wasn't hearing things again; at least he hoped he wasn't. He forced the thought out of his mind. This was his day. He shouldn't' worry about the voice.

"Mr. President! Mr. President!"

In the White House, President Brandon blinked, willing his eyes out of the thousand-yard stare so characteristic of his disease.

Camille had just entered with a large stack of leather folders. She put them on the resolute desk at which he now sat. "These need your signature," she said.

"What are these?" the president asked. The question was a reflex, not a true inquiry seeking an answer. He wasn't supposed to ask questions. He was just supposed to execute. This had been the agreement, the thing he had acquiesced to before they fixed things for him—fixed it so that he would "win."

Camille smiled a warning smile with eyes that weren't angry, at least *not yet*. "Joe, these are your executive orders. You're going to sign them for the American people, remember?"

"Orders?" He fingered the leather folders gently, then looked before him, just noticing a crew of ten reporters with sound booms and flashing cameras, waiting for him to act. How he had overlooked them he didn't know, but he suspected it had something to do with the disease.

Suddenly Camille's hand was on his. She whispered in his ear: "The American people don't know what's best for them. *We do*. We are going to help them. Remember?"

President Brandon looked at Camille. His instinct was to correct her because these things weren't for the American people. They were for the *other* people, the people who had printed the ballots, programmed the voting machines, paid the mules, and manufactured the virus. He was about to say so, but he still had the wherewithal to hold his tongue. For now.

He willed his trembling fingers to the top of the stack and pulled the first folder down in front of him. His movements were slow, painfully slow both for himself and his VP.

"Go ahead, Joe," she urged. She had replaced her face mask, not to protect herself or anyone else from viruses, but to hide the impatient look she knew she wore.

At last the first folder/executive order lay open. He tried to read it but could only make out a few words. "Gas" was one of them. Yes, this order would cancel the Keyway Pipeline and ban new fracking permits on federal land. This one would make the Saudis and the environmentalists happy. The last administration had stopped buying Saudi oil. Now the United States would be dependent upon it again.

The Saudis and the Greens had supplied a lot of money to rig the election in his favor. He owed them. He signed.

The next executive order stopped construction of the Border Wall—this was important. That needed to stop because a lot of his financiers were drug runners who wanted their routes to remain open through the southern United States into Mexico. He put his signature on the line.

But then he was tired, and the third folder he opened was unintelligible, a tangle of jumbled words his ailing brain couldn't unscramble. He put his pen back in his pocket, his reading glasses on his nose, then took his pen out again only to dislodge his spectacles from his face.

These repetitive, clumsy movements did not go unnoticed by the reporters who were tossing each other quizzical glances. One looked at Camille, his face a giant question mark. She turned quickly and put her finger on the signature line. "Here Joe," she urged, "sign here."

The president wasn't looking at the signature block but the sentence that had popped up next to it: *We know what you did last election.*

Startled, he jumped from the resolute desk and nearly tumbled off his leather chair.

Camille caught him by the arm, then turned her back to the press, whose camera flashes were now blinking so rapidly that the Oval Office looked like it was caught in a lightning storm.

When the president was stabilized, Camille whirled and announced to the media: "The president will now sign the rest of the executive orders in private!" This signaled the Secret Service, who formed a wall that pushed the press into the hallway, but they didn't go easily, and for several minutes afterward emotional protests filled the air outside.

When things finally quieted, the first lady found her way to Camille. "He had another episode, didn't he?" she asked in a rushed whisper.

The VP nodded, stealing a furtive glance at President Brandon, who by now was flinging folders violently from his desk. Soon the floor before the desk was covered, a small sea of leather at the edge of the oak. Meanwhile, the disoriented man behind it was breathing in shallow, mewling gasps. His eyes were once more were seized by the thousand-yard stare of dementia.

"What did he see this time?"

"He didn't say."

Jane let out a sigh. "Those orders are supposed to be signed by tonight!"

"I'll speak with our debtors," Camille told her. "I'll tell them we need more time."

Jane's lower lip sucked into her mouth and her sallow face drew tight. "These aren't patient people!" she hissed.

"No," Camille agreed, "but they aren't fools either. They knew about Joe's . . . *condition*. Heck, it's part of the reason he was chosen, their main advantage, but with every advantage comes disadvantages. He has spells, and with spells come delays. They know this. They'll wait."

"I hope you're right," Jane muttered, unconvinced.

Camille took the situation in stride. "Take the president to his bedroom and get him some rest. After he has a nap, I'll send a servant in with dinner. He may feel like signing then."

President Brandon heard the conversation and wanted to refute what they were saying but couldn't. The tragedy of dementia is that it casts doubt on everything seen, heard, and understood, everything except for one crucial fact: that its victim is ill, its victim is declining, and its victim is very much aware of that downward spiral. Having dementia is like

5

looking at yourself from the outside in, watching some inhuman spirit inhabit your mind and control your body and being powerless to stop the possession.

He remembered feeling like that then, as though he had separated from his body when his wife hoisted him up from the resolute desk. He remembered watching his wife escort an old, frail man from the Oval Office into his bedroom and smoothing the covers over him, but after this everything was a blank, a strange dark void, until an Asian intern opened the door of his bedroom. She was carrying a dinner tray.

"President Brandon?" the pretty intern asked. Born in the United States, Ma Song had no Chinese accent, but she did boast the slim figure and delicate features of the Chinese, which, incidentally, President Brandon preferred.

His strange loss of time was all but forgotten at the appearance of the intern with her slice of sirloin, mashed potatoes, and kale salad. "My, aren't you pretty!" he said what he thought. At seventy-eight, President Brandon may have had one foot in the grave, but his manhood was still outside it.

"Well, thank you, Mr. President," the intern replied professionally, as she set the tray down on his bed stand. She had just released the meal when the president's hand found hers and wouldn't let go.

The intern's eyes went wide with surprise, then dread. Ma Song had heard about President Brandon's ways with the ladies, but she hoped they were nasty rumors. However, his weathered wrist about hers—with a strength that didn't match its age—suggested otherwise.

"Mr. President, please, I have more meals to deliver. I must go."

But the president didn't seem to hear her. He leaned in quickly, his nose pointed straight for the crown of her head. *He likes to sniff women.* Ma Song remembered the stories about him with a hint of half relief. *He won't try to kiss me, just sniff me. Still. Gross.* She had to think of a way out of it. "President Brandon!" she exclaimed. "I didn't wash my hair this morning! I know . . . I know what you . . ."

The sentence ended with "like. I know what you like," but that isn't what President Brandon heard.

Instead, he heard *"I know what you did last election."*

This stopped him mid-sniff, and he locked eyes with the intern. Suddenly, she didn't look like the pleasant nineteen-year-old Ma Song anymore. No, she looked like *that girl*. That girl the Chinese had provided for him on his last trip to Beijing. He'd heard they killed her afterwards.

Suddenly Ma Song's porcelain skin rotted into a pale, ashen green that flushed sickly purple under the eyes and around the lips. A hole formed in the side of her cheek through which a set of rotten gums peeked; a worm inched its way from this hole and into his view. Her eyes faded into black holes.

She pointed at him with one arm, a skeletal arm with flesh hanging off in strips. "We, the spirits know," she said. "*We know what you did last election*. God knows. The American people know. Everyone knows. There is no escape from it."

At this, President Brandon leapt from his bed and tore into the hallway outside his chamber. The embellished portraits of George Washington, John Adams, and Thomas Jefferson all came alive, their eyes fixed on him. From the paintings, he heard the words: "We know what you did last election! We know what you did!"

He ran until he reached the end of the hallway, or what he perceived was the end. By then, his aged body was so flushed with adrenaline and his old heart so fully stressed that his mind, not optimal to begin with, was barely working. He ran into a wall adorned with a bust of Winston Churchill. The bust was just inches from the exit; it came between the president and his goal, toppling down on top of him. Miraculously, President Brandon caught it. He held the bust above his face.

"It's no use, old boy," said the bust, Churchill's characteristic cigar dangling from his lips. "We know what you did last election!"

The president screamed, not the scream a frightened old man would make, but a high-pitched, unearthly cry. It sounded like something that would come from a woman, or a prepubescent boy startled out of his mind. He flung the bust to the ground, and it landed at the feet of the Secret Service with a thud. Their hands were on their earbuds, speaking to the White House physician in hushed tones over their headsets.

"What happened in here?" Jane shouted at Ma Song, clearly blaming her for this recent spell.

The bewildered intern put her hands up. "I don't know! He just freaked out!"

And President Brandon was not done freaking out. By now the Secret Service men were approaching him. The White House physician had ordered them to restrain the president, and they were determined to execute.

Joe saw the Secret Service, but they were not alone. Others were with them, transparent ones in dated clothing. The head one looked like Abraham Lincoln, whose spirit was well known to inhabit the White House. Joe thought he had seen him from time to time, and his was the vision that most terrified President Brandon. For the whole country knew him as Honest Abe. Honesty was a quality that Joe had always struggled with.

"You're not real!" the president shouted, as Abraham stepped to the front of the Secret Service and knelt before him. "You're just another hallucination from that infernal dementia!"

"You're half right about that," Abraham said as he removed his top hat, "but you're also half wrong. Dementia is a disease that thins the space between this world and the next, allowing the person with it to see a little of what's on the other side and repent before they cross. But you haven't, have you, Joe? There's not an ounce of 'sorry' in you, is there?"

"I won!" the president whimpered as the spirit studied him disapprovingly. "I won that election. Now leave me alone!"

"No, Mr. Brandon. Your friends did a good job of making it look like you won. They put on a good show, but the truth always comes out—always. That's why I never bothered to lie." Abraham shook his head. "Lying is too much trouble. Speaking of trouble, you've caused enough. You're coming with us."

Camille entered just behind the White House physician, but both came too late.

President Brandon had collapsed, his body already cooling, his eyes open in a stare of pure terror.

The physician could find no pulse and began CPR while the Secret Service prepared the helicopter for airlift to Walter Reed Hospital, but they were just going through the motions. Everyone in that room already knew the president was dead.

At that moment, Camille was grateful for the mask she was wearing. It hid her expression of joy. She had expected to take over, but not so soon. What luck! What delicious, unbelievable luck!

The next day, President Camille Harold went to the Oval Office with a stack of yet unsigned executive orders. Expecting no problems, she invited the press in.

When everyone was seated with their cameras on, she opened the first leather folder. This one dealt with drug prices.

Ah yes, the previous administration had made insulin cheap for the American people—that wouldn't do at all. The drug companies had helped her get in. Now it was time to pay them back by making Americans last again.

Her eyes drifted down to what should have been the signature line. But instead of a nice blank bloc with an X at the beginning, there lay the words:

"We know what you did last election."

THE CAMEL REFUGEES OF HORSE RANCH

"**Y**ou can't coexist with animals who want to kill you!" Luka the German Shepherd exclaimed, slamming her artificial leg against the barn floor. This caused a layer of dust to fall from the white-washed roof and a boom to echo through the wooden rafters of the Animals' Barn. The obnoxious gesture also startled all the animals of Horse Ranch into silence. This was quite the feat, considering that until then the debate over accepting a camel refugee family had been quite lively.

All eyes then focused on Luka, each wearing a different expression.

The horses, the most plentiful animal at the ranch, blinked awkwardly before resuming their work on converting animal stalls to voting polls. They didn't like confrontation, nor did they understand what Luka was talking about.

The sheep stamped casually, then showed their behinds to Luka. They didn't have an opinion one way or another, at least not yet. They were still feeling out the crowd.

The donkeys Demi and Crate were openly sneering and disgusted—not at what Luka said, although they certainly weren't fans of it. They were more disgusted with Luka in general, but this was nothing new. They'd hated Luka for years.

Tex the steer snorted skeptically. Like Tex, the other steers knew what Luka was talking about, they just didn't want to believe it. Officially, they shared political power with the donkeys at Horse Ranch but rarely did anything of consequence, effectively letting the donkeys run the place.

The only animals taking Luka seriously were the pigs, whose IQ was a few points above the others, but whose numbers were the fewest. Their eyes were attentive, their snouts pursed thoughtfully. Mother Sow, Luka's best friend, stared politely while her piglet Junior played at her feet.

Luka was grateful for the attention, even if mostly negative. "As you all know, I have personal experience with camels. Some of the camels are good, but many want to kill us; it's too hard to know which camels are which. Therefore, I recommend accepting none."

Demi sneered condescendingly. "Luka! What a narrow-minded thing to say!"

"Oh, it's more than narrow-minded," Crate interjected. "It's downright *speciesist!*"

The word was like a bomb, like the Molotov cocktails Luka saw thrown at the troops overseas. It drew a stunned gasp from the animals. Eyes may have been on Luka before, but they absolutely bored into her now.

There was something odd about the word *speciesist*, some dark magic it possessed to turn those accused of it guilty without evidence. It worked its magic just then, and most looked at Luka with shock and disgust. After all, a *speciesist* was the worst thing an animal could be, worse even than being dead.

"Ah, *speciesist,*" Luka said. "Funny you should mention that word, because the camel's religious ideology is very *speciesist!* For one thing," the dog looked at Mother Sow, "they don't like pigs."

Mother Sow's son Junior looked up at Luka, then back at his mother. Mother Sow kept her eyes on her friend.

"They also don't like dogs," Luka continued. "I suffered a lot of discrimination when I served in Afghanistan. But you don't have to be a dog or a pig for them to hate you. Camels also consider animals who don't share their religious beliefs either useful idiots or cannon fodder."

"How bigoted!" Crate interrupted, rolling his eyes.

"Once they're here," Luka continued, "things will change in ways you can't imagine. Problems will surface that you've never dealt with—the kind of problems you *can't talk* your way out of!"

Laughter exploded from the rest of the animals because no one talked more than the donkeys, and everyone knew it. Usually they were masters of speech, making the ludicrous sound lucid and the crazed seem compassionate, but they had nothing to say just then.

"I think we've had enough debate," Tex interrupted. "It is time to vote on the matter."

"I concur with my colleague across the barn," Crate said, happy for a change of subject. "After all, the Animals' Barn exists for democracy."

In truth, very little democracy went on in the Animal's Barn. Mostly, the donkeys lived there—and very well, in fact. The painted white structure, with its solar heating, succulent hay, and ornate little windows, was far more luxurious than barns 2 and 3 below. The donkeys justified their lifestyle by calling their luxury structure the "Animal's Barn" and opening it up periodically for voting.

The horses started ushering all animals into a queue. Luka had just found a spot in the middle of the line when a horse came up to her, bringing news that the bear had passed Horse Ranch's borders again.

"Oh, Luka, you won't be able to vote." Demi's statement dripped with fake concern.

"She may move to the front of the line," Tex intoned wisely. "We owe her that much."

Luka nodded gratefully and trotted to the first poll, feeling Demi's eyes on her the whole way.

"Let us vote!" Crate declared, walking the line of waiting animals. "And in a way that honors the compassionate and non-*speciesist* history of Horse Ranch!"

Another gasp emanated from the animals. After all, a *speciesist* was the worst thing an animal could be! Worse even than being dead!

The next morning, Luka was sleeping off her bout with the bear when a familiar sound fractured her dreams; it was rumbling and loud, like an explosive, and the scent that chased it was acrid and sulfuric, like gunpowder. There was another scent, too, an earthy one that reflected the Middle East; Luka shivered at the memories it stirred in her and abandoned all hopes of further sleep.

The dog pulled herself into a sitting position and donned her prosthetic leg. The barn was mostly dark, with the faintest hint of purple peeking through the wooden boards. A shape shifted to her left; the noir silhouette belonged to a large beast, one slightly bigger than a horse. Its back curved up in a large slope before spilling into a thin and jagged neck that ended in a rounded head.

"Sorry, friend," the shadow said. "I am sorry to wake you. My name is Habib, and I need your help. I was told you are good with these things."

"What things?"

Another explosion went off before the shadow could answer, and the outside fully illuminated, spilling a golden sheen through the slits in the barn and revealing her mystery companion.

He was middle aged, with a large sagging hump and ragged fur. Upon his rounded head sat a small white hat with lace trim that fully concealed both ears. His large lips were drawn up in a nervous but hopeful smile, and his friendly eyes trembled. He anxiously glanced out the barn window. "Oh no!" he exclaimed.

Luka didn't ask what was wrong because she already knew. Camels were here, and if camels were here, then so were their traditions, many which involved explosions.

The dog dashed into the morning dusk. Another loud crash and blast of light greeted her as she cleared the barn. She shut her eyes against the blinding light and heat until she stood within feet of the ramshackle tack shed and the blazing fence surrounding it.

There, standing before the shed, was a female camel two-thirds the size of Habib. Most of her face was hidden by a head covering and veil, but her eyes were plenty angry. They locked with Luka's in a menacing stare. "Haram!"

"She said you are . . ."

"Unclean. That much I know. Habib, tell her I don't give a rat's butt what she thinks, I'm still in charge, and she can't set fences on fire!"

Habib translated this, then came back with "She understands and promises, but she still wants to set the explosives around the perimeter of the ranch."

"Whatever for?"

"Rival camel tribes," Habib explained. "You see, we are *Shati,* at war with the *Sanu.* Shasra is worried about protecting Horse Ranch from the *Sanu.*"

Luka face-pawed. "There are no rival camel tribes here, no *Sanu* within five thousand miles."

"She says not for long. The donkeys are bringing more camels. . . ." Habib broke off, his eyes slammed wide, and he turned back to his wife. The two of them exchanged several heated lines. At last, Shasra sputtered a camelish cuss word and turned away. Then, still fuming, she gathered up her detonation equipment and stormed off.

"What just happened, Habib?"

"My wife cannot speak English, but she understands some. She heard the donkeys talking about bringing in more camels." Habib's hump sagged along with the rest of him. "By Al, this is not good! I used to translate for the dogs like yourself in Afghanistan, and I was almost killed several times. I came here because I want peace. But not all camels do."

"No kidding," Luka panned. "We have to stop them."

"I will go with you."

When Habib and Luka arrived at the Animal's Barn, it was surrounded by almost all of Horse Ranch. The animals were bringing grievances to Crate. Demi wasn't around.

"The rancher always brings my food," Mother Sow complained, "but it was missing this morning!"

"As was my hay," mumbled Tex. "Most unusual."

"And we had less oats!" the horses neighed. The sheep were also bleating, even though they weren't missing food. They just wanted to complain.

"Are you certain?" Crate challenged condescendingly. "Maybe you misplaced your food."

"I am certain they did not, friend!" Habib interrupted. "No, the missing food is the work of my second wife, Sati. She steals things. She was the youngest of five daughters, so she was always starving. She started to steal food when she was a child and never stopped."

"So your second wife is a kleptomaniac?" Mother Sow asked.

"What is a kleptomaniac?" Habib asked.

"An animal who steals compulsively."

"Then yes, my second wife is, as you say, a kleptomaniac."

Crate was just a little behind things. "You have more than one wife?"

"I have three," Habib confirmed.

Luka's mouth pouched as she struggled to contain her laughter. Camels often had multiple wives. The donkeys, never having been deployed, were naturally ignorant of this.

"My second wife was a business deal," Habib elaborated after an awkward beat of silence. "I married her so her father would pay our way to Horse Ranch."

"Why didn't you tell us about your . . . *family situation,* Habib?" Tex asked critically, squinting one eye.

"You didn't ask," the camel replied.

Luka was beginning to like this camel. She could tell he didn't mean to be funny, but his raw honesty was delivered with effortless hilarity and hitting the others like a Mac Truck. Luka was loving every minute of it.

Crate realized something. "Where are your other wives?"

"My second wife is likely hiding the food she stole, and my first wife, Fati, is probably sleeping in. She likes to do that. There are no problems with Fati. We have been together many years."

"And your third wife?"

"KUFAR! KUFAR! KUFAR!"

The foreign word caused all animals to do a 180 pirouette in time to see a little piglet squealing for its life and making a beeline for Mother

Sow. The elder embraced her little one. "Junior! What are you doing here? You should be with your father!"

"I wanted to welcome her," Junior sobbed. "I even brought her a flower, but when she saw me, she screamed that K word at me. I don't even know what it means!"

Before Habib could translate the K word, a blaze erupted next to the Animal's Barn and quickly engulfed a small, standalone garage in which the rancher stored his tractor-trailer. Next to the garage was none other than Habib's third wife, Shasra, a cell phone in her hoofs.

"We just did this!" Luka yelled, advancing on Shasra. "I told you no fires!"

"You said *no burning fences*. This is a garage," Habib clarified, trotting next to Luka. "With Shasra, you must be specific."

"Fine. Tell her *no explosions of any kind*! No burning fences, buildings, or other animals!"

Habib translated, but Shasra had already lit the fuse to an IED she'd assembled while the animals were complaining. The spark quickly spread to the building, and the flaming walls of the wooden barn collapsed, revealing the tractor whose metal body was engulfed by the searing heat. The crimson flames reached their pinnacle brilliance when they hit the gas tank. Then a loud bang ensued, turning the vehicle into an inferno, and a tire sailed through the sky, landing in a smoking heap at Crate's feet. The smell of burning rubber was distinctive and damning.

"*Aloha Snackbar*," Luka sighed. "I just knew we'd end up with *Aloha Snackbar*."

"Our new residents are welcoming us with a barbeque!" Demi had just arrived from his morning walk and was rationalizing Shasra's pyromania in typical donkey fashion. "Cook some carrots while you're at it," Demi shouted. "Make sure they're vegan, would you?"

Shasra stared back with a look that was all but lethal.

Luka face-pawed. "This camel is testing improvised explosives, not making a friggin' barbeque!"

"Well, why did you say *Aloha Snackbar*? I mean, that literally translates as 'hello food.'" Demi giggle- snorted.

"Because *Aloha Snackbar* is soldier slang for . . ."

BOOM! Shasra may have stopped lighting fuses, but she also made no effort to extinguish them. Soon the fire found another IED placed just below the tractor. When the flames hit this, it turned the smoldering vehicle into a shrapnel cannon, pieces flying every direction of the clock.

"Incoming!" Luka exclaimed, pulling Habib down with her. The other animals let out a cry and rushed into the barn seconds before the jagged metal remnants found the roof.

Then passed a moment of silence, followed by neighs and bleats of surprise. Tex the steer ushered the animals back to barns #2 and 3 below, all the while assuring, "Don't worry, we'll sort this out."

Habib stood up. "Friends," he said to Luka and Demi, "now that Shasra has used her explosives, she may calm down. I will go and speak with her."

When Habib had gone, Luka turned to the donkeys. "We *just* voted on this."

"We did," Crate said.

"Everyone voted to bring them in," Demi added.

Luka cocked an eyebrow. *"Everyone?"*

"Well, except for *you* of course," Demi sneered. Naturally, Demi was lying. Luka knew this, as she knew Mother Sow and many of the steers voted *no*.

"OK," Habib, who had just returned, said. "Shasra is under control, but I'm not sure how long this will last. I do not have the same relationship with her as I have with my other wives because she was a blood deal."

Luka cringed. "I remember blood deals."

"Yes. Shasra's father said he would kill me if I continued to translate for the war dogs, but then I agreed to take his daughter off his hooves, so he did not. And everywhere we go, she tries to blow things up. She's very devout."

"She's not devout, she's oppressed." Crate doubled down on his trademark grin and disastrous narrative. "We'll get her a job. Then she won't blow things up anymore." He nodded smartly.

"Anyway, we're glad you're here, Habib, because we need your advice," Demi said, changing the subject. "We want to know how Horse Ranch can be more culturally sensitive to your kleptomania and pyromania. After all, we will be bringing more camels here soon."

Habib turned to Luka. "It is true!" He frowned severely at the donkeys. "Friends, that is not a good idea!"

"Why not?"

"Because I am agreeable and so is Fati, but many camels are not. My own brother killed my sister because she did not wear her saddle right, and two of my wives are crazy. As Luka can tell you, my country is wartorn and dangerous. It is because of the beliefs there."

"Camelism is just another religion," Crate protested.

"For many, yes, but for others it is politics and an excuse to kill in the name of Al." Habib shook his head sadly. "Please do not bring more, at least until my wives are under control."

But the very next week, Luka, Habib, Fati, and Mother Sow watched forlornly from barn # 2 as twenty camels were led into Horse Ranch.

"This is not good," Habib trembled. "I recognize one of them. Yes, the third one in the line! His name is Achmed, and he is from the *Sanu* tribe. He tried to kill me when I was helping the dogs, and now he is here! Other *Sanu* are here too! By Al, why?" he sobbed.

Luka looked at him. "Stay here!" she commanded and was soon in the donkey's faces. "We're supposed to vote on this!"

"We already did," Demi sneered, "and the vote was *yes*."

"For *one* camel family, not half of Afghanistan!"

"Well, that's your opinion, Luka, and what more could I expect from a *speciesist* like you?"

Luka's eyes narrowed viciously. That word had been overused, abused, and yielded to silence dissenting opinion until it had no meaning, and this was the most dangerous thing of all—a thing Luka could abide no more.

A growl rose in her throat, and she charged on the donkeys, barking insanely. "I will not be controlled with such nonsense any longer! I will call a spade a spade, an idiot an idiot, and a threat a threat! Speaking of threats, one of those camels threatened Habib because he translated for my kind during the war! He told me so himself. What's more, you brought in camels from *rival* clans!"

The donkeys stared at Luka, their eyes shallow and blank.

Luka called them out on it. "See? You don't get it because you've never been to war! You've lived in your ivory stable on the hill all your lives. Some of these camels can't live together—*they literally will kill each other* just for praying a different way! This place could look like Kandahar by tomorrow. The one positive I can glean from all this is the verbal gymnastics you'll have to go through to talk your way out of this—you tyrannical, elitist, cockwombles!"

Unbeknownst to Luka, the animals of Horse Ranch had followed and were watching her tell the donkeys off. A chorus of laughter erupted from all present, even the sheep, who until moments ago had cheered the arrival of the camels. The donkeys were horrified to find they had an audience, and for the second time in their lives, they could think of nothing to say. Luka had checkmated them for the second time. She was no longer just a nuisance: she was a threat to their power.

Something had to be done.

So, later that evening, the donkeys went to see Viktor the bear.

"You ask for me, da?" Viktor said when they entered the tree line. Viktor's mother had been killed by a rival male when he was barely out of cubhood, and he had escaped her fate by swimming from Russia into Alaska. Then, he'd trekked down through Canada to Montana, settling in the woods just outside Horse Ranch. He survived by fishing the streams beyond its boundaries and doing odd political hit jobs for the donkeys.

"We need the dog busy again," Demi said. "See, we're bringing these . . ."

"Camels, I know," Viktor finished. "I see today, like I see dog lose her mind over it. Not sure is smart, da? In Mother Russia, we bring camels, then camels bring trouble."

"We're not asking for your opinion, Viktor! We're asking for your services."

The bear shrugged. "OK, you the boss. I do. When you want?"

"Tomorrow when she's on patrol with the sheep."

"OK, keep busy or *more*? We discuss before . . . ?" Viktor leaned in and winked suggestively.

His hint was not missed by the donkeys; in fact, they were hoping for it. "Do what you must, Viktor. We've had enough of Luka!"

The next morning, Viktor caught sight of the herd and slowly approached them.

Luka saw him and immediately sprang into action. She'd dealt with Viktor before and thought herself able to handle him; she didn't know Viktor wouldn't be holding back today.

But another animal knew: Habib's favorite wife, Fati. Fati didn't like to sleep in as Habib thought. Fati liked to spy and gossip, especially on the donkeys, and she learned of their plans long before Viktor made his move. So Fati convinced Shasra to daisy-chain claymore mines along the edge of the forest where Viktor was sure to make his debut. When they were done, Sati arrived with snacks she'd taken from the new camel arrivals. And then the three wives waited.

When Viktor's bulky form slunk through the trees and tensed to sprint at Luka, Shasra blew the mines, sending a fiery wave roaring through the edge of the forest and turning its borders into a blazing inferno.

This stopped the bear, and the fire alerted *all* animals of Horse Ranch, to include the rival camels.

Achmed arrived on the edge of the forest and threatened Habib's three wives. The females responded in kind by shouting back. Shasra let fly several Molotov cocktails, and the opposite brood of camels started firing AK-47s. Cries of "*Al Akbar!*" filled the air, and a war broke out on the prairie, Habib's family with a few stray camels against others the donkeys had just brought in.

Viktor burst from the forest with his butt on fire and roared like a comet across the battlefield before landing in a trough of water along the fence line, but he had to abandon this as the fire spread. He soon disappeared into the edge of the woods, never to be seen again.

Demi and Crate emerged from their luxurious barn on the hillside and ran haphazardly into the battlefield. "Everyone, stop! You're oppressed!"

"Jobs, yes. We'll get you jobs! Then you won't be so violent!"

But the camels were so enraged by their ancient tribal feud that they didn't think twice about using their ammunition on the donkeys. After all, they had plenty. Within seconds the two political leaders of Horse Ranch were casualties of imported war, their bodies mere speedbumps that the tribes surmounted on their way to kill each other.

Most of the animals had run off, but the pigs, a few horses, and Tex saw Luka on the hilltop near the Animal's Barn and joined her. From this high point they watched the fire embolden, spread, then engulf the barns along with the corral and fence.

Habib soon joined them with Fati. His other two wives were still enjoying the war that the affair had morphed into. Their skirmish was consuming everything around them, and the hilltop animals stood in silence, powerless to do anything but watch.

Luka heard Mother Sow's soft voice. "You did everything you could to warn them." She saw the pain in Luka's eyes.

"Yes, is not your fault," Habib agreed, and Fati nodded for emphasis, her gauze veil waving in the wind. Like Habib's other wives, she understood English, she just couldn't speak it very well.

A somber mood descended on the hilltop animals, for the barns had burnt to the ground, the horse corral with its sweet grass was now a circle of embers, and the peaceful prairies on which the sheep and steer once ran now teamed with raging camels. Many animals were dead, their home was gone, and their way of life severely threatened.

But at least they weren't *speciesists*. After all, a *speciesist* was the worst thing an animal could be, worse even than being dead.

Glossary

Speciesist: animal version of racist

Aloha Snackbar: a euphemism for Allahu Akbar; means "Allah is Greater"

Kufar: a vitriolic name for animals or people who do not follow a certain religious ideology

Haram: unclean

REGARDING RIOTERS AND RABBLE-ROUSERS

Some men just want to watch the world burn.
—Alfred Pennyworth in the film, *The Dark Knight*

Rose City Riot

here were several things Chet liked about himself. The first was his hair, shaved on his left and flowing long over his right like a horse's mane. He loved to toss it during arguments and riots because he felt it intimidated his Nazi enemy. Chet was also fond of his clothes: black block laced with metal affixtures, and these chinked over his anarchy T-shirts when he walked, announcing his arrival in advance. But most of all, Chet treasured his intellect.

He was good at debate, and by debate, that meant shouting down anyone opposed to his nonconformist ideology. He was also intelligent enough to take on two majors: gender and Middle Eastern studies at Portland State University. He excelled at both while still finding time to help fellow antifa punch and intimidate Nazis.

It didn't matter that Chet couldn't translate Nazi or that his victims didn't fit this acronym's definition. Portland State antifa, Chet, and Chet's friends all believed Portland was filled with Nazis. Therefore, Chet and his friends dedicated themselves to cleansing the city of this evil.

One such friend was "T," a tall black youth with a set of dreadlocks as impressive as his height. Though born male, T considered himself transgender and was as particular about pronouns as he was about clothing. Chet never knew whether T would show up dressed as a male, female, or combination thereof. T had a spontaneity that Chet admired.

Chet's other friend Lizzy was short and plump, with an equally short and plump crop of hair on her head that she sprayed blue or green, but never dyed outright. Lizzy usually wore jeans and a communist T-shirt paired with a vintage jacket from the nineties grunge era. Her lipstick could be any shade from green to lavender, but never red or pink. Red and pink were conformist shades, and Lizzy was adamantly nonconformist.

One fall Sunday, the three met at a light-rail train stop on the outskirts of Portland. There was to be a gathering at Pioneer Square of Nazis, and Rose City antifa planned to show up in rebuke. Of course, the three friends eagerly volunteered, their rag masks and baseball bats ready to stop Nazis from doing Nazi things.

Pioneer Square was a large public space in downtown Portland with Greco-Roman columns oddly arranged for sitting, conversing, and the rare street performance. Once there, Chet and company saw that antifa were gathered behind a banner boasting red and black flags. A light October wind stirred their banner as they marched slowly forward. Police officers were present, both mounted and on foot. They held riot shields at the ready but mostly just observed from the square's periphery. Portland's mayor had a high tolerance for chaos and a soft spot for antifa; the police weren't going to move unless ordered to.

Random things were shouted: "Down with patriarchy!" "Western Civilization is a Disease!" "Go to Hell Nazis!"

That last phrase struck a note with the crowd, and soon the antifa were screaming, "Go to Hell NAZIs!" in unison repetitively. This litany was particularly ironic, as most antifa were vehemently atheist and did not believe in hell.

As though conjured by antifa's goading, the dreaded Nazis materialized at the opposite end of the square. This crowd wore all variations of red, white, and blue with mostly clean-cut—or by T's definition, *conformist*—hair styles. Unlike antifa, they didn't cover their faces. *Good*, Chet thought, *better to dox them later.* The Nazis varied in age, and though some were Asian or Black, most were of European descent. Chet rolled his eyes at this realization, simultaneously forgetting that he and Lizzy were white.

Chet looked at his friends. Unspoken agreement passed between them, and they ran to the Rose City antifa; the others made room for them as they tucked behind the banner. One said, "Welcome, comrades!" in between screaming "Go to Hell Nazis!" Then Chet and company advanced on their opposition with clenched fists and raised bats.

In return, the Nazis began shouting something about "liberty "or "freedom." Chet also thought he heard "hippie," but he wasn't sure. All he could think about was getting close enough to punch one.

At length his wish came true. The Nazis rushed the antifa, and all pandemonium broke loose. There was screaming, hair pulling, and plenty of punching. Chet's first victim was a woman, middle aged and blonde. She shrieked at the bloody nose Chet gave her, then ducked into the crowd.

Lizzy looked at Chet questionably, but he shook his hair with irritation. "A Nazi is a Nazi, Lizzy," he said. "Remember that!"

T agreed with Chet. In T's mind, the lines between many things had blurred: right and wrong, good and evil, male and female. In fact, the differences between these last two had faded so completely that he was no longer conscious of his natural biology or the PSI he was inflicting on his political opponent's neck. This opponent was a random biological female he had grabbed from the crowd.

Lizzy saw what was happening and peeled T off her. When he finally let go, the girl fell to the ground, slack, unconscious, and barely alive.

One of the female Nazis was an off-duty EMT. She shouted and cleared a spot in the crowd so she could work.

"Think it's OK to strangle women, do you? No friggin' sense of decency, any of you!" The man who said this was in his thirties with broad muscular shoulders and a crew cut. He looked like he did not belong in Portland, but had missed the plane to SEAL Team 6.

"Watch your mouth, Nazi!" Chet screamed, brandishing his bat.

"You wouldn't know a Nazi if one hit you!" the man countered in Chet's face.

"Do it and maybe I will!" Chet dared the man.

T was unaware of his strength as a biological male. The Marine was guilty of nescience also, but by virtue of his training, a training so richly ingrained in him that his next action was as instinctual as it was deadly. Suddenly, a punch had landed against Chet, a punch so effective that Chet didn't know what it had done to him, and he wouldn't for some time.

Lizzy screamed. T looked disbelieving at the Marine, then at Chet. Chet fell backward, then snapped back up. He smiled condescendingly and yelled: "I didn't even feel that!"

But the Marine wasn't looking at Chet. His eyes were downcast and focused on what Chet thought was the girl T almost killed. His expression was pure shock. His left eye twitched.

Lizzy and T dropped to the ground, obscuring Chet's view of the victims. Those with medical training were working frantically. Lizzy pulled out her phone and dialed 911.

Chet had no interest in this, but he wasn't going to judge his friends either. "I'll catch up with you later," he snickered.

No one acknowledged him.

Chet wandered through the rioting crowd, noting fists hurled and objects thrown. Half of the protestors were covered with eggs and half with blood. Baseball bats and bottles were plentiful. Someone set off a smoke bomb, and Chet moved through the mist toward a Black Nazi. Chet tried to punch him, but he avoided the blow and then ran away. Several other instances like this happened, causing Chet to wonder if he should work out. He was contemplating a gym membership when he felt a hand on his shoulder.

Chet turned to see three tall gentlemen wearing black slacks and brown shirts. Their blue eyes were burning behind impressively realistic skeleton masks.

"Gutten tag!" one of the skeleton men shouted enthusiastically.

Chet offered him a blank stare. "I'm sorry, I don't . . ."

"English, ja?" the second one tried.

Chet nodded an affirmative.

"We speak English!" the third the man said, offering his hand.

Chet shook it. "You guys from out of town?"

The three looked at each other and their eyes filled with mirth. "Ja, you could say zat," the first one laughed. He had a very thick German accent.

While this may have been a clue to some, the significance of their accents flew right over Chet's head. After all, Portland was proudly multicultural, and exchange students were the rule, not the exception.

"So, I was just punching some Nazis. You guys want to join?" Chet asked them.

"Oh yes!" the third man exclaimed gleefully, clapping his hands. "We love to punch ze Nazis!!"

"But first, introductions!" the second suggested.

"Ach, yes! My name is Rohm," said the first, "und zes are my friends, Gunter und Olaf." He pointed to the others who waved in greeting.

"Are you here with antifa?"

Gunter and Olaf dissolved into laughter, but Rohm said, "Not exactly . . . we have our own little . . . how do you say in English . . . *group*. We wear zes special masks, you see."

"Ja, everyone in our group has one," Gunter insisted, pointing to his face.

This wasn't a problem for Chet. "I love your masks. I'll wear one if you've got an extra!"

"Wunderbar!" Olaf jumped, clapping maniacally.

"Come then. The others are waiting!" The three men burst ahead, motioning for Chet to follow. On the way, they passed a line of mounted police officers. The police didn't react to their approach, but their horses turned wide-eyed to the passing men.

Gunter suddenly yelled, "Boo!"

The animals reared and dove headlong into the rioting crowd. They screamed hysterically while trampling several protestors underfoot. Two of the officers fell from their mounts. The third officer fared little better; he barely clung to his horse as it barreled through the melee.

Chet smiled. *Down with the patriarchy indeed, these guys are good!*

The three led him to a stairway that dove underground, one that was either part of the old, now defunct subway system or the Shanghai Tunnels. The public wasn't supposed to enter these *stairways to nowhere*, as the native Portlanders called them, but these men were the sort that made their own rules.

At the end of the stairway was a room that reminded Chet of a bomb shelter. It was concrete and cold with sparse lighting and stark furnishing. Seven men, all with the same brown shirts and skeleton masks, were seated at a long table speaking quietly amongst themselves. Rohm invited Chet to sit, so he did.

Olaf and Gunter followed suit and Rohm called the meeting to order. "All right, everyone, this is Chet, ja! And he likes to punch Nazis! In fact, we have seen his Nazi punching skills firsthand and recommend him for membership."

Chet tossed his hair proudly at the praise. Perhaps he had sold himself short earlier. These guys thought he had game!

"All in favor of ze new member raise your hand!" Olaf announced, raising his own hand. The men at the table copied Olaf; all seven hands went up.

Chet was overjoyed. "Thank you so much! I'm proud to be one of you guys, and I like your masks! By the way, when do I get one of those amazing things?"

"Soon!" Rohm declared. "Now, we have more pressing matters! Tonight, they come for us!"

"Who?"

"The Nazis."

"I knew it!" Gunter announced. "*Der Sturmabteilung* have become too popular!"

"Yes!" Rohm agreed. "Like all powerful men, the Nazis are afraid of losing power!"

Suddenly a crash sounded from above, and a shower of dust sifted from the roof onto the table. Rohm looked up, his blue eyes wide with panic. "They're here! Everyone, grab what you can and come with me! *Macht schnell!*"

Chet sprang up and turned to see a wall of weapons. Baseball bats, knives, and lead pipes sat like a riot dream stash before him. Chet didn't remember seeing the arsenal on the way in, but no matter. He had lost his bat after getting punched by that Marine Nazi, so he grabbed another.

The men spilled out of the meeting room and into a tunnel which led Chet to scratch his head, if only for a minute. Didn't he go down a flight of stairs? But he dismissed the thought and ran alongside his newfound allies until daylight greeted him.

Chet reached the tunnel's exit and stood still for a moment. It was just a moment, but that was all he needed to realize something was wrong. Pioneer Square was nowhere to be found. Neither were the tall buildings, the light-rail, or the rioting sea of black, red, white, and blue. Instead, the streets were cobblestone. The signs were in German. The houses were barely three stories high, and they resembled something out of a European fairy tale.

Townspeople were running and screaming. A group of men in black uniforms with red armbands were gathered across the cobblestone street, brandishing guns and knives at his newfound allies. They shouted something in German.

His masked allies shouted back, and as they did, one of the uniformed men fired a handgun taking out the seven Chet had met in the tunnel. Then, the gun jammed, and the men resorted to flying fists, baseball bats, and the primal insanity of humans determined to kill by any means necessary.

Rohm grabbed a man in a black uniform to Chet's left and punched him.

Gunter made a beeline for a uniformed man in front of a shop window and laid a solid chokehold on him. This was right after the uniformed man shot an old shopkeeper begging for his life. The civilian died with his eyes frozen in a look of shock and horror.

Another uniformed man came to his friend's aid and peeled Gunter off him, but not before Gunter managed to sneak in a solid left hook that bloodied his jaw.

As a stunned Chet was watching Gunter, another man in black tried to leg sweep him, but Chet cracked his bat against his brow. Enraged, the man came after him, arms outstretched, but Rohm bashed him over the head with a lead pipe before he could get to Chet. The man staggered and fell to the ground, stunned enough to no longer be a threat.

The pandemonium was real, but it was different from what Chet was used to and so . . . *ancient*. Something was very wrong.

Olaf put his arm around Chet. "Are you having fun, punching ze Nazis!?"

"These . . . these aren't Nazis!" Chet stuttered. "Nazis wear red, white, and blue!"

Olaf laughed. "Hey, Goebbel and Struesse!" he shouted to two men wearing black uniforms. They stopped fighting and looked at him.

"What is it Olaf?" Goebbel snarled.

"Ja!" the one named Struesse shouted, irritated. "We're on a schedule here!"

"Ja, sorry. It's just . . ." he pointed his thumb at Chet. "The new guy thinks you're not Nazis!"

The man Rohm had stunned looked up at Chet. Blood dripped from his mouth as he spoke: "That's hilarious!"

The seven skeleton men Chet thought were dead suddenly reanimated and raised up on their forearms. Their heads spun to look at him; their bony jaws hung open with laughter.

The Nazi holding Gunter hostage chuckled as did Gunter. The dead shopkeeper suddenly reawakened; he sprang from the ground like a zombie and cackled. The blood from his head wound careened down his face and into his mouth.

Goebbel gestured for a lead pipe, which Olaf willingly gave to him. Then he swung it squarely at the shopkeeper's head, separating it from his body and sending it flying through the air until it landed in the street. The head continued laughing despite severance from its vocal cords.

The whole village was snickering at an inside joke that Chet would soon be privy to. In some ways, realization had already creeped in. For instance, the masks Chet envied were not masks.

It wasn't a slow epiphany but one that hit him like a train, like the brown-shirted men were wearing masks one second and completely devoid of flesh the next. As Rohm laughed, Chet saw a worm wriggling over his teeth and his skeletal hands dabbing eyes unable to cry and a forehead unable to sweat. The rest of the men looked the same, pure skeletons in brown shirts half eaten by insects and evil, their bones dingy with death.

Chet's bat fell to the earth with a thud, and he stepped away from Rohm. He felt fear and anxiety, but no shortness of breath or racing heart. Come to think of it, he couldn't feel his heart beating at all.

"We were the Brown Shirts once," Rohm told Chet when the laughter died down. "Our job was to intimidate anyone who spoke up against Hitler or the National Socialist Worker's Party, and we enjoyed our work. After all, we were wicked men, just like you."

"And just like you, we punched innocent men, women, even some children!" Gunter added.

"Punched?" Olaf laughed. "That was the least of it!"

Rohm nodded. "You are right, Olaf. We did much worse. We ruined lives, businesses, and dreams." Rohm sighed, not with regret, but memory. "But then we grew too powerful, and Hitler turned on us . . ."

". . . and killed us during *Die Nacht der Langen Messer*!" Gunter finished.

"That is why, for all eternity, we must punch Nazis."

"And we Nazis must punch you back," said Goebbel.

"So true," Rohm acknowledged the Nazi. "We can only take a break from what you see when someone as wicked as us dies. Then, we may retrieve his soul from the physical world to join ours."

"Ja und Vielen Dank for bringing us to Portland!" Olaf gushed. "We loved Portland so much! That city was so angsty! So full of rage! So much like Germany in 1934!"

"Yes," Rohm agreed. "It was a wonderful break. But now we must return to reliving our deaths over and over again, in a loop that never ends through all of eternity!"

"But at least we get to look good, doing it, ja?" Olaf giggled, holding up a mirror.

In it, Chet saw his nonconformist clothes change into a brown shirt complete with German pants and swastika armband. His prized hair was thinning and white, and his eyes were blazing blue orbs hovering in stained yellow sockets. His bony jaw opened in a scream only hell could hear.

The ambulance Lizzy called eventually arrived. However, the crowd, which was too imbued with rage to part and too infused with hate to think, blocked its arrival for a full ten minutes. Those ten critical minutes sealed Chet's fate and put T's victim in a more precarious state.

When she arrived at the ICU, the doctors intubated T's victim and labeled her condition as *guarded.*

Chet was pronounced dead at the scene.

The Marine who had killed Chet stood somberly and waited for the Portland police to arrest him. T did likewise. Both held out their hands cooperatively as the officers placed their cuffs.

They were taken to jail where they shared a cell for the night. They spoke quietly, discussing anarchy, the US Constitution, and freedom of thought and speech without anger, or rage, or masks between them. T told the Marine that his real name was Timothy, but he hadn't said it in two years, as he wasn't sure if he could identify as Timothy anymore.

The Marine said his first name was Brian, but he hadn't spoken it in two years because, in the Marines, everyone goes by your last name. Deep down he'd wondered if he could identify as Brian anymore.

They learned how alike they were . . . in very *different ways.*

The following morning, Lizzy sat at a coffee shop waiting for a classmate. With one friend in jail and another dead, Lizzy was grateful to emerge from the Rose City Riot unscathed. She felt like she'd gotten a second chance at life, and she didn't want to waste it.

Her classmate Teri entered the coffee ship wearing a gray knitted beret and blue vintage scarf. A book on the Nazis, *actual Nazis,* was tucked under her arm.

German Words and Historical References

Nazi: National Socialist Worker's Party

Ja: Yes, pronounced "yah"

Macht snell: Be quick

Shanghai Tunnels: Tunnels under Portland where men were kidnapped and taken into slavery during the late 1800s to early 1900s

Sturmabteilung (Brown Shirts): This paramilitary group was infamous for helping the Nazis rise to power through intimidation of Germany's civilian population during the early 1930s. However, they were eventually disbanded by the Nazis. Many were also killed during the Night of the Long Knives.

Wunderbar: Wonderful

Vielen Dank: Many thanks

Black Lizards Matter

Unlike the other farm lizards, Tre De Lawn was neither black nor grey, but silver with black stripes that painted him from head to tail. His sparkling eyes were as golden and sunny as his disposition, and his argent cheeks were always gathered in a smile—for Tre was a happy youth with a good and honest soul. The tween lizard knew he was different from the solid grey and black lizards of his town, but he rarely considered it because his family told him not to.

"Your color doesn't matter, Tre," his mother Sally once advised with a smile that spread through her river-stone skin and sky-blue eyes.

His father Philip, a stately jet-black lizard, agreed: "Your mother is right, son. Your heart is what's important. In this garden, we treat all lizards the same." His father always seemed sad when talking about such things, and Tre couldn't imagine why. After all, Tre's garden community was Philip's philosophy in action: prosperous and peaceful, with all lizards tending the fields and bartering fairly with their neighbors. Though not without its troubles, farm life was good.

However, Tre's mother worried it was not enough. "Tre is too sheltered here, Philip. All he knows is our little community. He should see the city."

"I'm not sure he's ready for that." His father's sad voice was enough to draw Tre away from his homeschool lesson on communism. He peered through a hole in the floor of his room on the top of the hollowed-out stump that was his home. Below him was a funnel-shaped kitchen, complete with carved root shelving and dirt walls. His parents stood in the middle of the room.

"What if he goes with Old Lizard Williams?" his mother chanced.

Philip snorted. "Stubborn old reptile should have given up the city run years ago."

"Exactly! If Tre goes with Williams, he won't be alone, and neither will Williams! Every year we worry he'll break a hip in the city. If he does, Tre will be there."

Philip sighed audibly. "All right, as long as he stays away from the south side."

Tre leapt when he heard this. The big city! He had always wanted to go! In his excitement, he tripped over his history book, accidentally flipping to a lesson he passed a few days ago, one covering the odious Karl Marx.

"My veggies gonna rot waiting for your boy, Philip," Old Lizard Williams complained two days later as he stood in Tre's driveway. Philip and Sally had just finished loading their portion onto the cart, and Philip humored the elder by hollering after his son.

Tre appeared at his father's demand and smiled when his mother kissed him, but Philip pulled him into an embrace noticeably stronger than Tre was used to. "Be careful, son," he whispered.

"Philip, he's going to the city, not war," his mother chuckled.

"I hope you're right," Philip said when he thought Tre was out of earshot, but Tre heard and wondered.

For an old lizard, Williams proved surprisingly fast once he got going. The elder was like a car pushed downhill, gaining speed and momentum as the journey went on. Before Tre knew it, a sign greeted them: WELCOME TO LIZARDAPOLIS. From this point on the road turned from a crude dirt path into cobblestone lined with flowerpots, cinder blocks, and tin cans, things the city lizards used as homes. The little abodes were packed tightly together and stacked four or five high on one another, with not enough room to slip a tail in. On the roofs grew strange plants from which Tre detected a peculiar smell.

He wrinkled his nose at the towering stalks. "Mr. Williams, what is that?"

"Marijuana, boy," he replied. "City lizards grow marijuana, if they grow anything at all."

Giggles drew Tre's attention back to the thoroughfare. Several children had lined up alongside of the road, eagerly eyeing Tre's cart as he pulled into the marketplace. He thought they looked rather skinny, and their eyes widened as he parked his cart in a cinder block stall adorned with Christmas lights and solar lanterns.

No sooner had the country lizards set up than the gaunt youths offered their money. Alongside Tre other venders had similar experiences, and within minutes, the marketplace was filled with city lizards, frantically buying most of what Tre, Old Williams, and the other vendors had to offer. The polite customers moved with a sense of urgency and fear about them, stealing furtive glances over their shoulders as they browsed. They were also inordinately impressed with the produce.

One lizard remarked, "Wow, grapes! I haven't seen grapes in years!"

Years? Tre thought. He shot William a furtive glance, and the Old Lizard returned this with a look that said, *I'll explain later.*

When the day was almost out, Old Williams offered his thoughts on the matter: "This place has changed. We better pack up early."

"But we haven't sold everything," Tre protested. A quarter of their produce remained.

"Never mind that, boy. Just help me. We should get out of here before . . ."

"Before what, Old Timer? You realize you're in the wrong hood?"

Tre looked up to see two lizards his age smirking across the cart. One was bedecked with gold and silver chains, and the other wore a ballcap with sunglasses. Tre didn't like the vibes they were giving off.

"You two hungry?" Old Williams asked cautiously. "We got a few things left."

"We aren't interested in stolen goods, Old Timer!" snarled the youngest.

"It isn't stolen! We grew it ourselves!" Tre fired back.

The spectacled lizard removed his sunglasses and gave Tre a noticeable onceover. "Boy, you a black or a grey, cause I can't rightly tell?"

"Don't matter," his friend said. "If he's *with* a grey, he's a *sellout*!" The last word ended in a laugh, and his friend high-foured him.

"We didn't sell out yet," Tre protested. "We still have some left. We'll give you a good deal if you want it, since it's the end of the day."

"Shut up, fool!" the older barked, suddenly angry. "We don't tolerate his kind here, and I ain't sure we tolerate yours!" He put a hand on the cart and pulled forcefully.

Old Williams raised his cane and clocked the younger lizard with a speed that defied his age. He then went for the one wearing chains, but the bejeweled lizard saw Williams coming and tail-swept him. A loud crack resounded as the elder fell. "My hip!" he exclaimed.

"Little L! Dwayne! Why you fools wasting time with old lizards? Big C won't be pleased!"

The two youths froze and looked up in disbelief.

Tre followed their gaze to a beautiful she-lizard perched on the cinder block stack above him. Her scales reminded him of fresh soil mixed with coffee, the kind that grew the best produce. Her eyes were silver and sharp like dew on a month's wing, and her smirking lips were strawberry red. She looked a year, maybe two, older than himself.

"But Comrade Tanesha," the two protested, "We saw this grey and . . ."

"Wasted your time! Now go home, before you waste more of mine!"

The two youths took off into the fading light, and the beautiful she-lizard climbed down the cinder block. She frowned at Old Williams as he moaned on the ground. "We need to get him out of here. This place ain't too nice after dark." Tanesha pulled out her phone and called an ambulance.

"Take him to Healthy Scales North," Tanesha told the paralizards when they arrived. "His friend can come and get him in the morning."

Tre said goodbye to Old Lizard Williams and was soon alone with Comrade Tanesha.

The she-lizard strapped the cart to herself and started sauntering down the road. When she didn't hear footsteps behind her, Tanesha turned and grinned at Tre. "You better come on. It's like my family said, you don't exactly look like the other lizards around here. If the wrong reptiles find you . . . well, I'd rather that not happen, OK? Stay with me tonight—that is, if you don't mind sharing what's in this here cart."

Tre shrugged. "OK, ma'am." Tre had already taken a hefty profit. Sharing the remains seemed fair in exchange for a night of shelter.

Like Tre suspected, Miss Tanesha didn't live alone. Her home, or *pad*, as she called it, was a subterranean cutout beneath the city, not quite the sewer, but certainly not the subway or even urban apartments. It was as off the grid as one could get in the city.

Tanesha's "family," or *gang* more accurately, was crouched over long tables of a dry green substance that Tre's nose immediately identified as marijuana. Little L was counting copper pieces in the corner and Dwayne was arranging a small clutch of potatoes that didn't look like enough for a meal. They both scowled at Tre when he entered, then more eyes flickered from Tre to Tanesha, to the goods in the cart. Their gaze lingered longest on the latter.

"Comrade Tanesha, you never disappoint!" bellowed a deep, suave voice.

Standing at the end of the subterranean home was a large lizard wearing a crushed velvet jacket and several glittery chains similar the ones on Little L, only these were much more ornate. He also boasted a pair of sunglasses and cowboy boots that were platform and stately. A diamond tongue ring glittered as he darted this appendage, tasting the air.

"Hey there, Big C," Tanesha crooned, detaching from the cart. "I got you and the family a little score."

"I see that, but you brought more than a score." He looked at Tre.

"Oh, he's just a *inbetween* farming lizard, real ignorant of our ways. I met him out selling this here produce when, well, let's just say he realized he was in the wrong 'hood. But he don't mean no disrespect, Big C. He needs a place to stay. We can do that for him, can't we? 'Specially on behalf of all this food he gave to our cause?"

Big C removed his glasses and darted his tongue thoughtfully. His black scales gleamed as his amber eyes roved over Tre. "You look *real familiar*, boy. We ever met?"

Tre looked down; something about Big C made him uncomfortable. "I don't think so, Sir."

"Sir," Big C chuckled. "So polite. But I go by *Comrade*. We're all comrades around here—I'm just the big one."

Comrade! Tre's ears perked up. He'd heard that word before.

"Of course he can stay!" Big C said. He stepped up on a twisted root. "Comrades of the Black Lizards Matter movement, listen up! No one touches this *inbetween*, hear? He's our guest!" Big C plucked a ripe cherry tomato from the cart and tossed another at Tanesha. "Ya'll eat, then get into town and sell that weed, hear? And if they don't buy . . . well, *you know what to do.*"

The lizards rushed the cart and devoured the produce with a ferocity that unnerved Tre.

"Are they always that hungry?" Tre asked.

"Yes," Big C said, "because of grey lizards."

"Grey lizards?" As Tre looked at the cavern lizards, something occurred to him that hadn't before: they were all black. There was not a grey or mixed lizard among them, and Tre suddenly understood what *inbetween* meant. He wasn't sure he liked it.

A moment later the black lizards were gone, the marijuana bundles tucked under their arms as they spilled up through the tunnels onto the streets above, leaving Tre alone with Big C and Tanesha.

"I'm going to deposit our capital from our family's activity. Why don't you walk me out?" Big C told Tre. "Tanesha, you come too."

Shrugging, Tre trailed the boss lizard up a different tunnel into the moonlight where the little city was shut tight, sleeping. This section of town was like a dilapidated version of the market neighborhood. Cinder block abodes were plenty, but the road between them was missing large sections of cobblestone. The sad thoroughfare was also devoid of Christmas lights and lanterns, and there was a darkness here credited to something more sinister than the lack of electricity. It was like a spiritual void, an emptiness that Tre couldn't quite see so much as feel. The young lizard wondered what Tanesha's family was trying to fill it with.

"See this here?" Big C asked, gesturing to the ruin. "This is the result of theft, theft by grey lizards."

"They stole your crops?" Tre asked. "Sometimes bugs steal ours."

"They didn't steal our weed," Tanesha laughed. "Can barely get 'em to buy it." Her silver eyes were bright and smiling in the dark. Tre wondered how she could stay positive in a place like this.

"Did they steal the streetlights?"

"This hood never had streetlights."

"What did they steal?" Tre asked.

"Our *dignity*, they stole our dignity!" Big C shouted, irritated with Tre's questions. "The grey lizards have so much because they took it from us. We intend to take it back. "

Tre rubbed his chin thoughtfully; this all sounded awfully familiar. "How will you do that?"

Big C raised a clenched fist, and Tre noticed that Tanesha did the same: another familiar sign. "We, the black *prolizardtariat*, will seize the means of production from the grey lizards and distribute it equally among black lizards."

"Then, we gonna establish a paradise on earth, where no lizard will be hungry!" Tanesha chimed jovially.

"Those lizards in your cave seemed pretty hungry," Tre countered skeptically. "I'm not sure grey lizards are your problem, but rather your business model. From what I can tell the marijuana market is really saturated here. Perhaps you should try growing other crops. For instance, grapes? There's a big demand for them. It's the first thing Williams and I sold out of."

"Big, C, that's a great idea!" Tanesha cried. "Not that I don't like weed, but eating it all the time gets old, and it's not really all that fillin'."

Big C silenced Tanesha with a wave of his hand. The female lizard lowered her head and flashed Tre an apologetic glance.

Big C darted his tongue; a shadow of irritation passed over his face as he positioned his hands on his golden cane. He smiled, not a friendly smile, but a sinister expression that made Tre's blood run cold. "You know," Big C said slowly, "you sound just like your father."

Tre took a step back. "What?"

Big C brandished his cane. "You're Philip's boy, ain't ya!"

"How do you know my Dad?" Tre took another step.

"That old *sellout* left this hood to shack up with a grey lizard years ago, talking about farming this, and producing that. Using the grey lizard's system to get ahead."

"It's not a grey lizard's system," Tre protested, even as he retreated further, "it's the free market, and it doesn't care what color you are. It only cares about quality, supply, and demand."

Big C chuckled. "Tanesha is right, boy. You are ignorant. But you know, I'm real glad you stopped by. We always wanted to seize the means of production, but didn't quite know where to start. Now, we do know: *your little farm!*" Big C lunged at Tre, but the young lizard was too fast and darted through the crumbling infrastructure to where a jagged tree was growing amidst the buildings. Tre found north by reading its bark and took off that way.

Tre ran briskly into the night. For a while, he heard steps behind him, but they soon faded. The country lizard often ran long distances to chase away garden bugs, and he easily outpaced the communists.

In time the crumbling buildings gave way to straight structures, the broken roads to intact ones, and the pathways were lit once again. He ran until morning and then paused by a park fountain for a drink and a few hours' rest. A lizard out for a walk happily gave him directions to Healthy Scales North.

Tre took off toward the hospital but stopped when he saw a familiar purple velvet coat adorned with golden chains. Big C! He looked furtively to the left and right before turning into an elegant driveway lined with ornate statues and flowering plants.

Tre followed him partway down the drive. It didn't take long to see Big C's real pad, a large mansion made from the shiniest flowerpots and the choicest stones. Big C's lanterns were larger than Tre's father, and they glowed beside pools and fountains complete with Koi fish. Lush vegetation bloomed all around, from tomato stalks to plump grape vines. The vines were so thick that Tre remained hidden while Big C unlocked the mansion and closed the door behind him.

"So this is where he deposits our capital."

The familiar voice startled Tre, and he whirled to see Tanesha. Tre's cart was strapped to her back. Her silver eyes were large and hurt.

"How did you find me?" Tre sighed.

"I figured you'd come for your friend at the hospital. Also figured you could use this here cart to get him home if he couldn't walk. It's yours after all."

"Thank you for bringing it."

They were silent for a time. Then, Tanesha said, "Tre, if Big C hates greys so much, why is he living uptown among them?"

"Because Big C is a Communist, Tanesha. Didn't you learn about communism in school?"

"No, but I learned critical reptile theory."

Tre made a face as he looked at Big C's home. "Well, I studied communism. Communist leaders talk about seizing wealth for disadvantaged lizards, but they only seize it for themselves. They talk about distributing food equally, but all they distribute equally is poverty and misery. That's why Big C is living like this while the rest of ya'll are hungry. And as for him hating greys . . . well, he obviously doesn't hate them that much if he's living here. He's using that to control you all, keep you focused on them while he does this and who knows what else behind your backs. I suspect a lot of what you brought home went to fund his lifestyle. That's why food is such a problem for your family."

"So, Black Lizards Matter isn't really about helping black lizards?"

"I don't think it ever was."

Tanesha nodded sadly, then her eyes widened with realization. "Listen Tre, we need to get you and your friend home. I know Big C; he meant what he said about your farm!"

The two parked the cart near the hospital, then quickly entered the tall cinder block structure. Old Lizard Williams was in a chair on the third floor with a fresh bandage on his right hip. He brightened when Tre and Tanesha entered the room.

"Boy, I'm glad to see you! The doc said I can leave anytime."

"Good, because we need to go. Tanesha and I will explain on the way."

Within minutes, Old Williams was discharged and on the cart. Tre pulled while Tanesha guided them through the twists and turns of the city. Within a few hours they were just shy of the marketplace, and there the stately flowerpot homes and stone high-rises gave way to dilapidated shadows of themselves—fractured ruins flaming from newly set fires.

The streets before them were torn up, dotted with potholes that jolted the cart and nearly twisted Tanesha's ankle. Christmas lights lay on the ground, sparking from disrupted circuits and wires. A shiver of glass struck Tre's paw, and he looked down to see a rainbow of the shattered stuff below him.

Weeping and smoke filled the air. Several panicked lizards scurried past them, their children on their backs, their goods in their arms.

Tre soon saw why. Tanesha's family materialized through the smoke like ghosts—hurling pebbles at windows and digging their claws into the cobblestone road to upend it. A brawl had broken out between the family and several grey city lizards. Little L and Dwayne were actively punching one on the ground.

Dozens of other black lizards took notice of Tre, Tanesha, and Williams then, crawling out from under the broken cinder blocks, slithering from the shadows like dark spirits. Their eyes were on Tanesha and her companions as they closed in, encircling them.

"Hello Tanesha." Big C appeared between them and the melee, his hand on the hilt of his cane, red tongue darting. "You aren't turning your back on Black Lizards Matter, are you?"

Tre froze, but Tanesha leapt in front of her new friends, trembling with anger. "You turned your back on it first!" She reached down and ran a claw across her tail, revealing a patch of silver.

"Whoa, she a grey!" Little L shouted out.

"I'm *inbetween*, fool!" Tanesha corrected. "And ya'll down here are starving while big C is living uptown with greys!"

Hesitation and doubt flickered across the faces of Big C's entourage. They looked at each other, then at Big C. Meanwhile, Big C remained stone faced and solemn, his face betraying nothing. Tre thought he must be an amazing poker player.

"'Stead of terrifying city lizards and breaking stuff, why don't you bust up this mansion of his? He built it with capital he said would go to the movement!" Tanesha brandished her phone on which were pictures of Big C's secret. "Here's proof! You got anything to say, Big C? Or are you just gonna stand there, blaming other lizards?"

"He'll just stand there," a sad voice interrupted.

Tre looked up. There behind the Marxists was Tre's farming community, led by his father.

"Philip, it's been too long," Big C laughed.

"You never did learn how to work for a living, Chris."

"Chris?" Tanesha exclaimed with the other lizards from the family.

"That's *comrade* to you, Philip! You old *sellout!*"

"Doing right by yourself and family isn't selling out, it's stepping up. If ya'll had any decency, you'd know that. I've got a fruitful garden—you've got destruction and weed. I've got peace and prosperity—you've got rage and victimhood. That's why I went to the country, where the only scales lizards care about are weigh scales."

That was the most Tre had ever heard his father speak about color, and as he did, Tre noticed for the first time how colorful his neighborhood was. The farming lizards behind Philip were black, grey, and every shade in between, as were many other lizards. Some Tre didn't recognize.

"Who are they?" Tre asked Tanesha, gesturing to the unfamiliar reptiles surrounding Philip.

The female lizard hung her head. "The city folk my family been roughing up."

"I think you pushed them too far," Tre said as the two groups engaged. What followed next was as much an ideological clash as it was a physical one, one of freedom against oppression, capitalism against Marxism, and personal responsibility against victimhood. It was good versus evil, culminating in a battle of tail, claw, and fists.

Unsure of what to do, Tanesha and Tre hung back, but Old Lizard Williams, busted hip and all, sprang from the cart and charged on the BLM Marxists with his cane a blazing. He quickly found a member of Tanesha's family and sent him crying into the depths of the city. Then he turned on Little L and Dwayne with a revenge beating that sent them away, too.

Minutes later, when the country and city lizards had declared victory, they detained the remaining members of Tanesha's old family and did something they had always been afraid to do before. They called the police.

When the cops arrived, Tre caught up with his father, who had lost Big C during the fight. He was staring into the distance, contemplative and sad.

"You two knew each other?"

"He was my best friend once, but we developed irreconcilable differences."

Tre darted his tongue thoughtfully. He wanted to know more about the relationship but decided against asking. His father looked too sad. "Do you think he'll be back?"

"*He* may or may not be son, but *what he stood for will be.* Classic Communists use wealth and poverty to divide lizards, but ones like Big C use jealousy and scale color. These things always come back, son. The trick is recognizing them when they do."

Regarding Covidiocy

A time is coming when men will go mad, and when they see someone who is not mad, they will attack him, saying: "You are mad. You are not like us."

—St. Anthony the Great

Conspiracy Cat

"**S**oon the humans will all wear muzzles and be chained to their homes by their great, glowing boxes!"

This announcement by Chester the cat stopped the weekly meeting of the pets of Sunny Side Street cold—not because they were surprised by Chester. He was, after all, the neighborhood conspiracy cat. Known for making odd announcements about aliens, lizard people, and government plots for totalitarian control, Chester was a well of odd machinations, most of which he shared at inopportune moments.

He even wore a tinfoil hat that each week boasted another layer of the shiny kitchen essential. It rose then above his awkward eyes, awkward because his right eye was twice as large as his left and constantly watering. Also, his nose continuously twitched. Indeed, all of Chester seemed to shudder, an endless nervous tick that Chester insisted was the result of aliens shooting electrical energy through his body.

"Uhh, Chester," said Tommy the tortoise, "that's weird, even for you."

"*Weird* doesn't begin to describe it!" Chester said, his tremor intensifying. "When the humans don their muzzles, they will isolate themselves. Then you will see them *change!*"

"But why would the humans wear muzzles?" laughed Bonnie the collie.

"The muzzles will restrict their oxygen. All organs, especially the brain, rely on oxygen. Oxygen restriction will limit the humans' ability to think critically and question the obscene.

"Also, forcing the humans into social isolation will alter their brain waves," Chester continued. "Oxygen deprivation coupled with social isolation will launch them into a state of psychosis, making them vulnerable to suggestion. Then and only then will they be willing to surrender their civil liberties to the government and undergo *mass pharmaceutical experimentation!*" This was said with great emphasis, and Chester stood on his hind legs, his front paws in the air, his tinfoil hat slipping over his head.

Tommy the tortoise, Rocky the Labrador, and Bonnie Lass the collie all looked at him, aghast.

A siamese kitten named Misty said, "You're crazy!"

Chester looked at her with his large, watering eye. "Don't worry about my mental health, little one. Worry about your human's!" And with that, Chester launched himself dramatically over the back of the fence, leaving the other animals of Sunny Side Street speechless.

The next morning, Tommy the tortoise walked into the kitchen. His human, a middle-aged, single, portly gentleman, was looking at his laptop, but in a strange sort of way. The screen was positioned so that all Tommy could see were his human's eyes. They were unusually large, liquid, and fearful. His human almost didn't look like himself.

The tortoise shook his head. He must have misinterpreted his human on account of hunger. Yes, that was it, he thought. So, Tommy sauntered over to his bowl, expecting to see the usual offering of carrots and baby spring greens. Instead, it lay empty; another unusual finding, and one that simply wouldn't do.

After all, Tommy was hungry.

He smacked the bowl with his foot, clearing a metallic ring, then looked at his human, who was still staring at his computer screen.

The tortoise sighed, then smacked the bowl again, but more forcefully. This time, his human looked up, and Tommy caught his breath.

Covering his human's mouth and nose was a large, unsightly strip of cloth: *a muzzle!*

Across the street, Misty was having a similar experience. Her human, a twenty-something female yoga instructor, was sobbing herself senseless on her futon. She'd started off by soaking her pillow. Then, she'd grabbed Misty, drenching her fur and holding her with a grip that almost sent the cat running behind the washing machine—*almost.*

Misty resisted the urge for two reasons: (1) her human needed her, *really needed her,* and (2) Misty was curious (not an unusual state for a cat). There was something very odd going on here. Her human was talking about never being able to see her boyfriend again or work as a yoga instructor again and how something was going to kill her.

But Misty didn't quite hear what that something was because her human's words were slurred by tears. "No more parties every again, Misty! No more fun! I want to die!"

Wait a second! Misty thought when her human said that. All of these things had one thing in common: social isolation. Her human was afraid of social isolation, just like Chester had foretold!

Two doors down, Rocky the Labrador and Bonnie the collie were sitting and watching a great glowing box. Their humans, a married couple, were seated on the couch behind them, letting out the occasional sigh or gasp of terror.

"Have you ever heard such a load of crap in all your life?" Rocky asked Bonnie when they were halfway through the broadcast.

"Well, it's CNN, so . . ."

"They're trying to scare the humans to death," Rocky continued, "over a virus with a 99 percent survival rate! And just look at our humans, wearing muzzles! Don't they know viruses float right through those things? It's like using a chain-link fence to stop a mosquito."

"Yeah, muzzles don't do anything, just like the animal version."

Rocky cocked his head at the glowing box. "I don't know about that Bonnie," he disagreed.

"How so?"

"Muzzles *do* do something. When I wear one, I can't bark or whine very well. I also feel submissive and easier to control . . . wait a second!"

The dogs looked at each other.

"You don't think?" Bonnie said.

"What? That Chester was right?"

Bonnie didn't answer. She looked back at the glowing box and Rocky followed suit. They watched the CNN newsman drone away about a vaccine the humans were rushing through for the better part of five minutes before Rocky said, "I think we need to have a special meeting. We can't let this go a week. Besides, and I can't believe I'm saying this—I want to know what else Chester knows."

When Chester appeared before the animals at the special meeting the next day, his reception was much different.

At his arrival, the gathered pets quieted immediately and parted with a bow, as a crowd before a president or dignitary. All eyes were on him, transfixed and curious.

The cat noticed their behavior but didn't' alter his. He merely sidled up to his normal place atop the fencepost and adjusted his tinfoil hat, waiting for Bonnie or Rocky to call the meeting to order.

But this time, no one called the meeting to order, no one began speaking, and all eyes remained on Chester.

"What?" he belted at last. He wasn't used to quiet. He was used to sneaking his theories in between everyone else's statements.

"Well," Rocky began awkwardly, "we were wondering what your next prediction is."

"Yeah, like which stocks will go up." Tommy was joking, mostly to cover his distress. His human had been very devout about muzzle wearing over the last two days, and it disturbed Tommy greatly. He missed his human's smile.

Misty, who had called Chester crazy at the last visit, was much humbler this time. "We want to know what's going to happen to the humans, Chester. Mine has been crying for two days straight."

"Mine won't stop watching their glowing box!" Tommy exclaimed.

"Mine either! How do we stop this, Chester?" Bonnie asked.

"Yeah! What's the lizard people's end game?"

"All right, everyone, quiet down!" Rocky interjected. "Let Chester answer!" The Labrador nodded up at the conspiracy cat. "Go ahead, Chester."

Chester looked at the troubled animals. He felt bad for what he was about to say next, but it had to be said. For all his faults, lying wasn't one of them. "The end game of this unethical social experiment was not devised by the lizard people, although they are involved. No. Big Pharma and the US government are the main players. They want to create a more obedient human being."

"But why?" Misty squeaked.

"Most of human energy is spent trying to control other human beings; it has been this way since the dawn of human civilization. Some humans are as addicted to power as they are caffeine. Right now, humans with this addiction control the seat of power in the US and the world.

"As for the *how*," Chester continued, "the humans will further descend into madness. You will see them don two muzzles and cover their eyes with plastic! Then, they will begin speaking to their glowing boxes! Watch for it! When it happens, you will know they are one step closer to agreeing to the experiment!"

And Chester exited as dramatically as before, falling backward into the ground behind the fence, his tin foil hat tumbling after him.

Just as Chester had predicted, the humans began to wear two masks, then cover their eyes with clear plastic.

Tommy's dad put a hood over his eyes until he looked like a welder. Now, not only did Tommy miss his human's smile but the love from his human's eyes as well.

Bonnie and Rocky's humans had a thick pair of plastic glasses that fit over their regular eyeglasses. They wore these most of the time, except when they took them off to talk to their glowing boxes.

Misty's human stuck with one mask, but she was an emotional wreck. She talked to her glowing box, or rather, cried to it. She spoke of things that would make a psychiatrist cringe, let alone a kitty like Misty.

It was so bad that Misty took to hiding the sharp objects. By the end of the week, there was a large collection of knives stashed under her bed.

By the next meeting, the animals were on pins and needles to hear what Chester said next, but to their surprise Chester didn't speak, except to introduce a small white rat he had brought with him.

"Hello, my name is Hal," said the rat. "I'm a former lab rat, and I'm here today because humans took my jab." He laughed at his little joke.

"He likes puns!" Chester exclaimed.

"Hello, Hal," said the other animals.

"It's great to be here," said Hal. "I'd like to share with you what I learned while working for Big Pharma. On average, it takes a billion dollars and eight years of rat, then monkey, then human research to bring a drug to market. I should know, I've seen a lot of drugs . . . taken a lot of them, too. So if I forget what I'm talking about midsentence, you'll forgive me. "

As if on cue, the rat stopped, blinked, and then smiled at the crowd. "Hello, my name is Hal."

"You were just talking about bringing a drug to market," Chester redirected Hal.

"Oops, that happens from time to time folks, my apologies. I've taken a lot of experimental drugs."

"Yes, you said that also," Rocky said.

"Anyway, this new vaccine coming down the pipeline didn't get that same testing. They're pushing it through at breakneck speed."

"How breakneck are we talking?"

"Eight months."

Shocked silence followed Hal's admission, the type of silence in which one could hear a pin drop. The animals looked at each other.

"So, what you're saying is that the humans will be doing the testing instead of rats," Misty said.

"Yep, the humans took my jab," Hal laughed.

The little kitten blinked, then reached behind her fluffy body and put a pink tin foil hat on her head. She'd made it just in case she heard further confirmation of the lunacy the world was descending into. Hal's admission was just such a confirmation.

"Hal, any idea of what this vaccine will do to the humans?"

"Several companies tried for twenty years to push the mRNA vaccines through and failed. There were . . . *safety concerns*."

"Like what?"

"Oh, not much," Hal said, "just autoimmune disease, organ failure, prion disease, infertility, myocarditis, endocarditis, miscarriage, dysmenorrhea, blood clots, nervous disorders, and . . . uh . . ."—Hal tapped his chin along with his memory—". . . oh, yeah! *Sudden death*!"

"What in the actual hell?" Tommy yelled. "And the humans are going to line up for that? I refuse to believe it!"

"That's where you're *wrong*!" Chester said. His right eye was watering and his body trembling again, his tin foil hat rocking gently against the orange tufts of fur on his head. "The glowing boxes will dump fear on the humans, driving them more insane by the day, until they are willing to do *anything* to end it. This includes shoving unproven chemicals into their bodies."

"OK, that's it!" Bonnie yelled. "We've got to save these idiotic humans from themselves. I know it's a tall order, but we've got to try! Chester," she yelled at the cat, "can't the aliens help us? The aliens that send all those radio waves into your body? Don't they have anything to say?"

Chester looked at her, startled. Then a wide smile spread across his face. "That's it!" he exclaimed. "The glowing boxes are giving the humans directions, like the aliens wire mine through my hat into my body. The glowing boxes will tell them how to participate in the pharmaceutical experiment. So . . . we have to *burn the glowing boxes!*"

The animals were nodding enthusiastically at each other. Then Rocky spoke: "OK, Chester. We're with you!"

The next night, the animals stole matches from their kitchens, shredded cardboard, and lit a large bonfire in the center of the cul-de-sac at the end of Sunny Side Road.

Then, they chucked the TVs, computers, tablets, and all other manner of glowing boxes into the leaping flames. With each piece of mind control that entered the bonfire, it grew higher until it attracted the attention of Misty's human, who woke at 2 a.m. and called the fire department.

Tommy's human ran out to look at the scene and started talking to Misty's human as the fire trucks arrived. It turns out that Tommy's human was looking to lose weight and had always wanted to try yoga but was too embarrassed to join a group on account of his weight.

Misty's human agreed to give him private classes.

Bonnie and Rocky's humans were the last to realize that their glowing boxes were missing but weren't distressed by it. "I have a feeling they're feeding us a load of crap, anyway," the husband said to the wife, who agreed. Then they spread out lawn chairs to watch the firemen do their work, the first bit of propaganda-free entertainment they'd enjoyed in a while.

Chester's human was an elderly lady who didn't have a glowing box, only a small cell phone. She waved hello to her neighbors as she rounded the electronic fire with Chester on her heels. She wasn't wearing a muzzle, and when the other humans saw her without one, they removed theirs, too.

The animals saw Chester's lady enter the bushes at the end of the cul-de-sac, Chester trailing behind her.

Misty, Rocky, Tommy, and Bonnie looked at each other.

"Isn't Chester's human elderly and nearsighted?" Tommy pointed out.

"Yeah," Misty said, "and she's going into the forest!"

"We should follow her," Rocky said.

So they did, down a sloping ravine until they came to a clearing in which an odd-looking humanoid figure with large black eyes and grey skin was standing before Chester's human.

The animals gasped in unison: *an alien!*

"Well done," the alien said. "But you know you can't save them all."

Chester's old lady removed her glasses and straightened up. When she let her hair down, she looked twenty years younger. "That's not my goal, Lord Zlorp. Chester and I only need to save a few for the dominoes to fall against the Globalists and their New World Order."

"Let's hope you're right. We'll be in contact." And the humanoid figure turned toward a glowing dislike object that suddenly appeared behind him. He entered the craft; seconds later, it zoomed into the sky and disappeared.

The animals turned to one another, silent and shocked.

Misty smoothed the tin foil hat on her head.

Chester saw his friends and padded over, smirking gently. "What do you say, guys? My human and I can't do this alone! And after all, today's conspiracy theorist is tomorrow's prophet!"

As Chester was speaking, his human approached and knelt before them. The animals could see clearly that she wasn't elderly at all, but middle aged with auburn hair; she had been wearing a disguise!

She offered an outstretched hand to the animals. In her palm was a stack of tiny, pet-sized tin foil hats!

An awkward moment of silence followed as the pets stared at the hats. Then Bonnie tentatively stepped forward and removed one meant for her. Before placing it on her head, she noticed a strange electronic device in the cone of the hat outfitted with a soft, flashing green light. "Wait, these aren't just foil?"

Chester smiled smartly. "Of course not. They're communication devices! We put them in tin foil hats so the government thinks we're nuts! That way, they leave us alone!"

"It's like hiding in plain sight," his human chuckled, putting a tin foil hat on herself.

"You speak animal?" Tommy the tortoise exclaimed.

"A gift from the aliens. But enough about me. Chester will begin your training." She nodded at her cat. "Go ahead, dear. There's no time to waste."

"Right!" Chester declared and jumped up on a rock. "Now raise your right paw and repeat after me:"

I am the Conspiracy Crew. I predict freely and factually in the hope that my predictions may never come true.

I never desire to be proven right—only wrong, by my own paw if possible.

I will not seek glory for myself but for the One who sent me. I will not seek salvation for myself but for the ones I serve.

I am a tool against the evil of the New World Order, but I am only one of many. The ultimate tool is truth, and I will seek it relentlessly and unapologetically, no matter how absurd it may sound. I will endure ridicule from many for the deliverance of even a few.

I am the Conspiracy Crew!

DELILAH THE BRAVE

"**L**ocking the meadow down is the only way to fool the hunter!" said the leader of the deer. He was called Dr. Foxi by the others, due to his degree in human studies and anthropology. The large buck had an impressive rack of horns and a booming voice to match.

No deer was said to know more about humans than Dr. Foxi, and this is why the whole herd was gathered around him, listening to his every word. Their home, Deer Meadow, was a remote place in the thick of the Kansas wilderness. The only building was a small human cabin at the far edge of their meadow, but even that had lain empty for years.

That was until a truck rolled up next to the cabin two days prior and flickering lights lit the aged home. Human voices were heard from within, alternately whispering and laughing. The original estimate was two adult humans, but recent deer scouts had seen two young ones, too.

It was a true emergency.

"What does *lockdown* mean, exactly?" Thrasher, the lead deer scout, asked.

Dr. Foxi gave him a severe look. "It means we all stay in our nests. No playing, no morning walks, and especially no gathering. It will attract the humans' attention."

"That's an awful lot to ask."

"Half the herd will die if we don't do this!" roared Dr. Foxi, and this cowed further opposition. The rest of the meeting was spent discussing the details of this "lockdown."

Delilah, a small deer recently out of fawnhood, stood in the back of the crowd, watching the scene unfold. She was at that delicate stage best compared to human adolescence, but her tiny legs still resembled a fawn's, and when the sun caught her coat just right, faded white spots were still visible. However, within her young body lay an old soul, one genuinely concerned with what she was seeing.

Something about the whole thing was off. The "lockdown," the fear Dr. Foxi was inspiring, and worse, every deer's reaction! All of them were fixated on Dr. Foxi. Their ears were cocked, absorbing every word, and their eyes, which looked more like pools of fear to Delilah, were large and almost worshipful as they gazed at him. True, he was an expert on human behavior, but he wasn't a god. They were looking at him as if he was, and it disturbed her.

When the meeting disbursed, Delilah found herself alone in her nest, where she was to remain until Dr. Foxi said otherwise. She was too old to go back with her mother and too young for a mate, so like many her age, she remained alone.

She did everything she could to keep her mind occupied. She counted the leaves around her thicket, then arranged and rearranged some stones ringing the sides. She peeled the bark off a tree and stacked it up into a little squirrel house in hopes that one would come and sit by her, so she could have someone to talk to. A couple squirrels did come by, but they didn't stay.

Two weeks rolled into two months, and then a third. Delilah saw no hunters, but she did hear a lot of weeping from the neighboring thickets.

The fawns cried because they couldn't go to deer school or play.

The mother deer cried because their babies were so bored and miserable.

And the deer Delilah's age cried because they couldn't rut or find mates like they should be doing this time of year. Delilah swore she heard every deer cry at some point, and as time passed, the weeping got worse.

One morning, Carver, a former classmate of Delilah's, turned up dead. The body was found at the bottom of a cliff just at the edge of the meadow. From a distance, his body looked contorted and mangled, as though he had endured a fall. Thrasher had found him, and Dr. Foxi appeared next to the body almost instantaneously along with the rest of the deer, who were excused from the lockdown just long enough to see Carver.

"Aha!" declared Dr, Foxi. "The hunter has claimed his first victim!"

Delilah cautiously pushed her way through the crowd while Dr. Foxi was speaking. Her tiny frame enabled her to get close without anyone noticing her. She felt a stab of pain while looking at Carver because he had been a good friend to her during deer school, but she stamped the feeling down. She had no time for emotions; she needed to figure out what was going on and fast. She leaned in close for inspection.

When she did, she discovered that there were no bullet marks on his coat. Furthermore, why would a hunter leave Carver's carcass? Wouldn't he take the meat home and eat it?

Delilah took a whiff, and when she did, she smelled no human odors. Instead she smelled sadness, fear, and surrender.

This death wasn't from a hunter. No. Carver had committed suicide.

Just as Delilah reached this conclusion, Dr. Foxi noticed her. With a disapproving snort, he pushed Carver's body into the river.

The lockdown was growing more and more unpopular by the minute, so Dr. Foxi came up with a plan to give everyone a little more freedom.

"We will all weave coats out of tree branches and wear them. This will camouflage us from the hunter and allow us to graze."

"What about deer school, or mating?" Thrasher asked.

"No, still too dangerous!" exclaimed Dr. Foxi, snorting at the very idea of them enjoying life.

So, the deer wove foliage coats and passed a mandate that no deer could leave their thicket without such a covering. The coats allowed the deer a little more freedom, but there were disadvantages to them. For one thing, they were itchy and uncomfortable. For another, they felt heavy and restrictive. The little fawns couldn't leap or play in them, and they made foraging a chore for everyone.

Still, any deer who didn't wear one was shunned or attacked by the others. "What are you doing, you selfish deer? Do you want us all do die?" was a common confrontation coatless deer suffered.

Delilah hated hers, and that hatred only intensified the more time that passed without seeing the hunter. In fact, to this date, she couldn't think of one deer who had encountered this threat that had upended their lives. She began to wonder if he even existed, and so she decided to find out for herself.

One night after the first snowfall of winter had blanketed the land in an inch-deep span of white, Delilah left her nest and shook off her coat so it lay outside her thicket. Then she set off true north in the direction of the hunter's cabin.

It was around nine o'clock by human hours when she stopped to assess her progress. The moon was not yet full but high enough to light her way and bathe the forest in a silvery sheen. Delilah recognized the tall sycamores and great oaks lining the path on the way to the hunter's cabin. She'd come this way on a field trip in deer school some years ago during the section on human studies. Delilah remembered that from here, the trees only grew taller and thicker until parting at the cabin.

She took a deep breath and entered the thick path. She had only gone a few feet when she heard a sharp screeching above her—metal grinding on metal.

She stopped, sniffed the air, then looked up at an eerie sight. From the tallest tree hung a half-secured metal chair. While the ladder portion was still firmly anchored to the tree, the seating was pitched forward, hanging over and angled sideways. It drooped over her like the talons of a vulture or the teeth of a wolf. Then the wind caught it again, slamming it back against the tree, only for it to pitch forward and hang quietly as the breeze died once more.

Delilah's instinct was to run, but she chose bravery instead. Something wasn't right, and she was going to find out what.

She took a few steps forward, then hit something warm and moss-like just below the snow. She hesitated, then poked the strange object with her hoof.

A moan came up from the snow. Someone was buried alive!

Delilah dug frantically with her hooves and snout until she unearthed a human clad in a soft flannel covering that she had mistaken for moss. He had a dark beard that hid most of his face, but his lips had a blueish tent as did his eyelids. Delilah put her ear to his chest and listened for his heart: it was slow but steady. He was alive—barely.

Despite what Dr. Foxi had said about humans, he didn't look dangerous. On the contrary, he was the one in danger, in danger of freezing to death.

What could be done? Delilah thought for a moment. She was too small to drag him to his cabin, but she might be able to save him with her body heat. If she did, she could find out everything she needed to know about hunters.

When Delilah woke the next morning, the hunter was sitting upright, his face a mask of shock and wonder as he stared at her.

Delilah was brave. "Good morning," she said, "I'm Delilah. You fell out of your tree stand and I found you nearly frozen to death on the ground, so I laid down beside you to keep you warm."

"Yeah," the hunter said, looking at the half-secured tree stand still swaying in the breeze. "I remember falling asleep, then the next thing I know, here you are. Thank you."

'You're welcome," said Delilah, shaking the snow from her back, "but I didn't do it for free. I want something from you in return."

The hunter laughed. "I wish I could give you something, but I don't have much these days."

"Not material goods; *information*. I want to know all about human hunters. If you tell me everything I want to know, I'll consider your debt repaid."

The man brightened at this. "Well, that I have plenty of. What do you want to know?"

"Your name for starters."

"Roger," said the hunter. "It's Roger." And then Roger told Delilah that not long ago, he had owned a restaurant in the city that was shut down on account of some virus the government went nuts over. They closed a bunch of small businesses—Roger's included. He was supposed to reopen, but that didn't happen. He lost his ability to support his family, then his home, until the only thing he had left was this hunting cabin and surrounding land willed to him by his granddad.

"I thought," said Roger, "that I'd come live out here for a while. Really, that cabin is all I've got left, that and my truck. I've got a little money—not much. But if I shoot one big buck, that will feed my family the whole winter and into the spring even."

"So, I'm too small?"

"Not to offend you, but yes. Besides, I could only afford one buck tag this year, and you're a doe."

Delilah blinked. "I'm sorry, what's a *tag*?"

Roger thought the best way to explain the tag system was by taking Delilah to Walmarket, the nearest store that sold wildlife hunting tags. After a brief shower at his cabin and introductions to his relieved family, he strapped Delilah into the passenger seat of his truck, but not before putting an old hunting dog's vest on her.

"This way you look like my therapy animal," he said of the vest.

"Therapy animal?"

"Yeah, some people with depression get therapy animals. Makes 'em feel better to have a critter around. Anyway, therapy animals can go into stores while regular animals can't."

Delilah thought of the squirrels she had built a house for and wondered if they qualified as her therapy animals; likely not, she decided.

In the Walmarket she got a few odd stares, but humans weren't supposed to ask questions about other human's therapy pets. "It's considered rude," Roger explained. So the unlikely pair walked unaccosted to the back counter, where an adolescent human was staring wide eyed at the deer, who immediately set to asking him about the tag system.

It turns out the tags cost money, which was something Roger didn't have a lot of. One tag meant one deer per hunter, and then it applied only to certain types of deer. Roger's tag was only good for bucks, so if he shot a doe or a fawn, he could get in trouble with the human authorities.

Speaking of shooting fawns, the rules were clear.

"That's almost never allowed," the adolescent at the counter said as he shook his head vehemently. "Even if it was, I don't know a hunter in this town that would shoot a baby."

"I know I couldn't," Roger agreed; "just something wrong about shooting a fawn."

"But that means they've got the kids isolated for nothing!" Delilah exclaimed.

Both humans looked at her quizzically.

"I'm sorry," Roger remarked. "What's that?"

Delilah shook her head. "Nothing." She grabbed a free pamphlet on the tag system from the bewildered clerk. "Listen Roger," Delilah said, her mouth full of pamphlet, "I've got to go. Can you take me back to your cabin now? I'll find my way home from there."

Roger quickly obliged, and after a brief goodbye to her new friend and his family, Delilah was off like a shot through the thick forest and into Deer Meadow. The 2020 tag guide was firmly in her mouth; she was beyond excited to show the herd what she had learned.

She meant to find Dr. Foxi and have a word with him before anyone else, but when she got to Deer Meadow, she saw Thrasher first, wearing his knitted foliage coat and watching the other deer rotating turns for grazing.

"Delilah, you left your nest?" Thrasher said, bewildered. "And where is your coat?"

"Never mind that! Gather everyone, it's important!"

"No gatherings!" said a familiar, authoritative voice. "Or the hunter will shoot us all."

"No, he won't!"

"How do you know?" asked Thrasher. By then a group of fawns were tentatively gathering, their expressions a mixture of hope and curiosity. Their mothers were close behind.

Delilah could see that she had their attention. "He won't shoot us all because he can only shoot one buck. That's all he needs, and that's all he is allowed! The humans have this system called the tag system. It helps them conserve wildlife. See!" Delilah proudly slapped the paper on a rock in front of her and anchored it with her hoof. "They never shoot fawns, so the kids can go to school and play again! The hunter at the cabin can't shoot does, only bucks, but just one buck because he can only afford one tag."

"Rubbish!" exclaimed Dr. Foxi.

"No! It's all here, in human language! Go ahead, read it!"

Delilah expected Dr. Foxi to at least give the paper a passing glance. Instead, he raised his hoof and violently ground the guide against the rock, shredding it to pieces.

"I won't have you sharing false information here, Delilah. Staying hidden and down is the only way to avoid the hunter, not indulging in some teenage deer's fantasy of a return to normal life."

Delilah froze. Seeing the paper decimated by Dr. Foxi's hoof filled her with shock. He hadn't even looked at it. A supposed human expert had not shown any interest in actual human literature. This could only mean one thing.

"You're no expert, you're a control freak!" Delilah growled for all to hear.

Dr. Foxi's head angled down as he charged at Delilah, but she turned quickly and ran back through the forest, past the broken tree stand and the path of thick oaks and sycamores to the only creature who understood or believed her: *the hunter.*

Roger was splitting wood outside his cabin when Delilah arrived. He waved a greeting. "More questions already?" he laughed.

"Just one," Delilah panted, "and it's more like a clarification. You told me you need one big buck to feed your family. *Just one?*"

Roger propped his ax against a stump. "Just one."

"Good. I've got the perfect one for you."

"I really can't thank you enough," Roger said to Delilah as he loaded Dr. Foxi's lifeless carcass into the back of his truck. "This is quite the deer. Now I have everything I need!"

"So, no more hunting?"

"Not for deer. Now, spring turkey, on the other hand," he laughed. "I can't guarantee that." Roger started back to the cab of his truck but hesitated. He'd lit a small fire to keep warm while he prepared Dr. Foxi for transport "I should put this out."

"Please don't. I need it for something. I'll put it out when I'm done. I promise."

"All right, just be sure you bury it real good. Forest fires are no joke."

Delilah watched Roger's truck amble away. When it was out of sight, she filled her lungs and called out to the rest of the deer. It was a loud, raucous call, that of a mother deer crying to her young. It was meant for the children. She wanted to get the fawns out first.

They came, followed by their mothers. At last, the older males appeared, then males and females Delilah's age. All were still wearing their coats and expressions of wonder and confusion.

"It's safe everyone," Delilah announced. "The hunter is gone. He won't return until next winter."

"How do you know?"

"Because the hunter is no different than a common predator. As you all know, predators only eat certain kinds of food and never take more than they need. Turns out, one cruel politician is all he needed."

There was a pause at this. Then Thrasher said, "Where's Dr.Foxi?"

"He's no longer in charge," Delilah explained, not wanting to share grisly details in front of the fawns, but the adult deer understood and breathed a collective sigh of relief.

A little fawn crept next to her just then. He was wearing a foliage coat far too large for his small frame and struggling to move in it.

Delilah grabbed it with her teeth and cast it into the fire.

The rest of the deer looked at each other, then one by one cast their coats into the flames until they were no longer burdened by weight or fear. Slowly they began to talk to each other again, but their voices were still low, their actions hesitant. They kept looking at Delilah.

Finally, Thrasher said what they were all thinking: "What should we do now?"

Delilah smiled. "Anything you want!"

The Apartheid of the Swamp

One hot Florida day a meth lab exploded, blowing out the wall of the drug dealer's single wide trailer and killing the criminal chemist instantly. The explosion also decimated his fish tank, spilling his pet piranhas into the tributaries of the neighboring bayou. Amazingly, the fish were unscathed. More amazingly, they seemed changed after the accident, sporting faster fins, sleeker bodies, and bigger appetites.

Ravenous, they tore through the water, eating anything that moved and some things that didn't. They ate schools of fish, cranes, and raccoons that came to the water's edge. They gnawed fishing boats until the crafts capsized and the humans in them were fending off the creatures in the water. One fisherman was lost to the rogue pets, but he wasn't the only large victim.

Several elderly and unsuspecting alligators were performing water aerobics in the morning bog when the carnivorous fish came upon them. A senior named Merv had just submerged below the surface for a stretch when the cruel fish snagged three of his swimming mates, taking huge chunks out of them until they were no more.

Merv suffered a bite or two but managed to escape. Despite his age, Merv was in good shape, as was his wife, Marjorie. The couple sped past the gator guard Dwight and Reggie, his young trainee. The two were surprised by the speed of the elderly, their panicked voices, and the heady smell of fear following them, so rather than reprimand them for disrespecting borders, Dwight and little Reggie followed them into the center of Gator Glade.

"Ya'll," Merv panted on arrival, "we got ourselves a problem!"

The other gators looked up from the mossy banks as Marjorie and Merv collapsed on the shore. "Mutant fish are in the bayou!" Marjorie exclaimed, presenting her right back leg with a large, pink bitemark.

The other gators gasped and ran to the elderly couple. Panicked voices filled the air when they realized three of the gators from the water aerobics group hadn't made it back.

Steven Bartholomew stepped the front of the crowd. He was the only gator to attend and graduate from Gator University near Disneyworld, and everyone called him "Science" on account of his fancy school learnin.' "Mutant fish, you say?" He examined the elderly's wounds.

"Yes, sir! They had these teeth, see, and they came right at us, a chompin' and a growlin'. Least, I think they growled. It was all so scary!"

"We barely got out alive!" Marjorie elaborated. "Clem, Clancy, and old Josephina didn't!"

"Why didn't you eat them?" Dwight said. Unlike the rest of the gators, he was still floating comfortably in the bog with young Reggie— thoughtful, strong, and unafraid.

The question was like a bomb going off; it silenced the crowd of chattering gators and drew all eyes toward Dwight for two reasons: (1) the other gators weren't used to Dwight speaking, because he was a strong, silent-type gator, and (2) his suggestion sounded ludicrous, even dangerous! Who ever heard of eating a mutated fish?

In the thick of this silence, young Reggie's parents Gerald and Wilma realized he was still with Dwight, and they barreled toward their young'un, yanking him onto shore and shooting a suspicious glance at Dwight as they did so. Little Reggie's face fell as he waved goodbye to his mentor.

Their dagger eyes unnerved Dwight, as he had always considered Wilma and Gerald good friends, but Science spoke up before he could ruminate on this too much.

"I'm sorry," Science chuckled at Dwight. "What did you say?"

"I said, if they was fish, why didn't they eat them?"

"Because they was mutant fish!" Marjorie explained. "All mouth, and all teeth!"

"Were they bigger than a gator?" Dwight persisted.

By then, Merv was annoyed. "I say, boy, didn't you hear a thing we said? They was mutated fish. *Mutated!* You can't eat mutated fish!"

"Merv is absolutely right," Science purred. "Who knows what will happen if we eat mutated fish!"

"Hear! Hear!" Mayor Crassy agreed. "We must fight these fish another way. And I think Science is just the gator to find it."

"He certainly is!" Merv and Marjorie agreed, with a chorus of gator cries following behind them. Wilma and Gerald chimed their agreement while Reggie crouched between them. He sent Dwight a silent but meaningful shrug while his older brother Samuel blinked with concern.

Dwight didn't say anything but felt something evil afoot in the air.

That evening a mandate went out from Mayor Crassy confining all gators to the riverbanks of Gator Glade. This was to keep them safe while Science investigated. Excused from the mandate were Science, as he had to be free to work, Mayor Crassy, because he was the mayor, and Dwight, so that he could guard the other two.

Science determined that his first step was to study what had mutated the fish. Thus it was that the trio found themselves at the site of the water aerobics attack. There, they detected a strong, acrid smell.

"Meth!" Science coughed the word.

Mayor Crassy held his nose. "How did the fish get ahold of methamphetamine?"

"I'd guess humans," Dwight cut in. "I know of a Florida Man trailer down the way what cooks it. I recommend we check that 'un out first."

Science nodded. "Lead the way."

And so Dwight did, but when they came upon the place Dwight remembered, they found only a fraction of the structure remaining. It had been reduced to half a trailer, really, with the thin walls buckling in on themselves, like an old orange peel curling as it rotted. A few wires sparked within the structure, and from the ruin Dwight perceived the same toxic methamphetamine smell.

"Careful," Mayor Crassy cautioned, as he gingerly stepped onto the bank. But despite his caution, he ran his foot into a shard of glass, which led him to cry out and Science to rush to his aid.

As Science plucked the glass from the mayor's claw, Dwight followed the shard to another and another until he perceived the husk of an aquarium too large for so small a trailer. A small tributary led from it to the bayou.

"This here looks like where the fish came from," Dwight said. "Maybe they ain't so much mutated as just . . . not native to this area. See, humans do all kinda funny stuff, like take animals what aren't supposed to be in a place, and bring 'em there. For example, my cousin Jethro lives with a human."

"Preposterous," Science said.

"No, it's true. Jethro still lives down the way with a human named Jeremiah. Feeds him all kinda human foods and marshmallows."

"Not that," Science snapped. "I was referring to the idea that the fish weren't mutated." He pointed at the shards. "This methamphetamine clearly led to their mutation. I can engineer a repellant from it."

"Excellent idea!" Mayor Crassy congratulated. "Why, I hope you can get to work on it right away." Several more jubilant sentences flowed between the two gators concerning this.

Meanwhile, Dwight stood there with his mouth open and his head reeling. He knew he was a simple gator, but he couldn't have heard right, so he tried to clarify: "Ah, beggin' your pardon," he interrupted, "but did I hear you say you're gonna use meth to make the remedy? The same thing you think what *mutated* the fish, you're gonna use to . . . *repel* the fish?"

"Yes."

Dwight blinked reflexively. Several thoughts echoed in his brain, none of which seemed polite enough to say, and as his mind rehearsed different, more diplomatic options, Mayor Crassy grew impatient.

"I say, Dwight, what exactly are you getting at?"

Dwight looked down at his paws and the sparkling shards of glass mixed with meth. "I never seen any good come from meth. Humans get crazy and lose their teeth when they take it—I seen it on my patrols—I can't imagine it being too good for us either. I think we ought to eat the fish."

"This again!" Mayor Crassy sputtered. He turned to Science. "As soon as your remedy is complete, we'll make it available to every gator. And you," he scowled at Dwight, "no more talk about eating those mutant fish, ya hear? In fact, I hereby proclaim that no gator is allowed to eat these fish *ever!*"

When the other gators heard Mayor Crassy's proclamation, they obeyed. Even Dwight obeyed. He didn't seek the mutated piranhas out, and when they appeared he didn't try to eat one. He just chased them away and warned the others.

Meanwhile, the rest of the gators eagerly awaited the completion of Science's remedy. When it was finally done and mass produced, they didn't hesitate to take it. Of course, the elderly gators got it first, on account of them being elderly and more at risk for a brush with the mutated fish. Then the middle aged like Wilma and Gerald, and then the young. Within a month, every gator who wanted the treatment could get it, and all took it, except for the baby gators, as the mutant fish hadn't gone after them yet.

But there was one holdout adult gator: Dwight.

"You don't want protection from the mutated fish?" all the jabbed gators asked. They thought Dwight rather odd for not taking it.

"Beggin' your pardon," he'd answered politely, "but I'm the biggest gator in the bayou. Way I see it, I'm already protected. I don't need that fancy drug."

The other gators shrugged and thought him odd but left it at that . . . *for a while.*

As soon as the last eligible adult gator got done with his poke, there was a large celebration at Gator Glade. For the first time in weeks, baby gators, grandma gators, and all gators went swimming in the water. The morning water aerobics for the senior gators even returned, and Dwight was again allowed to take young Reggie out for patrols.

The jubilance was real and palpable, but it was not to last.

Three short days after the celebration, Dwight was out with Reggie by a boat. Now this Florida Man had brought with him a big old bag of marshmallows, which he dumped into the water upon seeing the gators, along with a happy Florida Man greeting. Reggie and Dwight were just gobbling the fluffy treats when a fish head bearing unnaturally large teeth popped up in front of Reggie. "Uh, Dwight," Reggie said nervously.

No more had Reggie spoken than the water was filled with dozens of fish heads teaming on the surface, their teeth chomping and gleaming ferociously. Dwight rolled himself forcefully between Reggie and the school of mutant fish. "Get to the glade!" he ordered, and as Reggie took off, Dwight turned to follow. As he did, one of the fish clipped his leg. With a cry, Dwight rolled and kicked it off, propelling himself through the water with his tail. As he cleared the scene of the attack, he heard the Florida Man cry out: "Piranha!" and fire several shots into the water.

Dwight had never heard the word *piranha* before and wondered what it meant.

At the glade, things were no better.

Marjorie and Merv had been attacked again, as had Wilma and Reggie's brother Samuel, but thankfully there were no fatalities. Reggie's father Gerald was waiting with a scared look on his face when Dwight nudged his protégé onto the bank and into his father's arms.

"Turns out the fish like marshmallows, too," Dwight tried to joke, but the punchline fell flat, as all the gators were so shaken up and disappointed that despite their efforts with Science's fancy drug, the fish had still come, and the fish had still eaten.

A meeting was called, and several possibilities for the attack were offered and debated. Dwight thought the most sensible came from Reggie's brother Samuel: "Maybe the drug doesn't work?"

But the other gators didn't agree. On the contrary; they became downright irate at the suggestion. *Science's chemical not work? Unthinkable!* A dozen hisses and boos were thrown Samuel's way, so much so that the teenage gator shrank behind his parents and disappeared into the brush.

In the end, the gators did decide upon a reason, and the reason was that not all eligible gators had taken the medication. Dwight's name surfaced, and every reptile turned to him.

Though he was the biggest gator in the glade, Dwight felt as though he were shrinking under their stares.

"You're attracting the fish." Science said what all the gators in Gator Glade were thinking. "But you can change that. We have a dose for you, Dwight. You can take it." He held the syringe out with his claw.

Dwight looked at it, then at the gators before him. It was then he noticed something he hadn't before: they were all missing teeth, and some more than others. Even Science himself was missing the whole front row, and Dwight knew why. They had all taken the drug, a drug engineered from meth.

"You don't' want to get eaten by mutated piranhas, do you, Dwight?" Merv said, accusingly. He was missing the most teeth of all. "Or get us eaten?"

"*Don't you want to follow Science?*" Marjorie asked.

"No," Dwight told them. It was the hardest *no* Dwight had ever said, but he had to be true to his beliefs. That, and he didn't want his teeth to fall out.

"You're a selfish gator, you know that, Dwight?" Merv growled. "You'd put yourself above the whole glade!"

Few things got Dwight angry, but that did. "Ya'll say I'm attracting the fish, but ya'll got attacked same as me, when I was in the open bayou far away from this glade! Way I see it, this has nothing to do with me. Now I ain't saying the drug doesn't work, I'm just not convinced it does. And I'm worried about losing my teeth. If ya'll looked in the mirror recent, you'd see you've lost some of yours." Dwight paused at that, but none of the gators looked at each other or checked their reflection in the swamp like Dwight thought they would.

Disappointed, but undeterred, Dwight continued: "At the end of the day, I got to do my job. If that drug causes my teeth to fall out, I can't! So maybe I'm a tiny bit selfish, but only so I can continue to work for the rest of the gators here!"

But logic is irrelevant to a mob and of even less significance to a cult, and the reptiles of Gator Glade were in the full grips of both. They were about to maul him when Science stood up suddenly and said, "Now, we don't know for sure it's Dwight. It could be the baby gators."

For you see, the baby gators hadn't taken the medication either. Giving rush engineered remedies to adult gators was one thing, but giving it to juvenile gators was quite another. A long pause fell over the congregation while they pondered these things; it was enough to disarm the mob, if only for a moment.

Science took advantage of it. "All the same," he said to Dwight, "the rest of us would feel better if you stay far away from Gator Glade. You know, just in case."

So it was that the apartheid of the swamp was born, with Dwight ordered to isolate himself in the dense reaches of the tall water tupelos and black gums on the shore opposite the river feeding into Gator Glade. If he saw humans, he could still report it, but he had to shout out from six feet or more away from any other gator.

The days were easy, as there was always a Florida Man about for entertainment, but the nights got lonely. He passed them by praying, listening to the crickets, and watching the fireflies dance. Unfortunately, his peace was often broken by the screams of gators across the way in response to another attack from the fish.

His first impulse was to get involved, as he knew they were all missing teeth and unable to fight back like he could, but then Dwight remembered the hard apartheid under which he now lived and the uncleanliness the others now associated with him.

While Dwight endured his quarantine, Science reformulated the remedy for the baby gators. Now, Dwight didn't know about this last part. He'd heard it mentioned before his apartheid, but he never imagined his community would take it that far. They wouldn't give a rushed treatment to baby gators—*would they?*

All ethics aside, the drug was pint size and doled out to the young before you could say *marshmallow*. Most of the young'uns did well, but some were less fortunate. A weak heart and breathing problems sometimes followed the injections, especially in male gators. A few even died. Naturally, the parents got concerned, but their concerns were tempered.

"There is no correlation between a weak heart and the remedy!" Science insisted, following the claim with a long speech about how heart problems were common in young gators. He was not only a good chemist but an excellent orator—so excellent, in fact, that the other gators believed him despite evidence to the contrary.

Therefore, the injections went on until Reggie's brother Samuel fell victim to one, leaving Reggie to dread his fifth birthday. For then, he would be old enough for the remedy and possibly the same fate as his brother. That he couldn't abide, and so on the night before his birthday, he secretly made his way across the swamp to Dwight's edge of the swamp.

Upon finding his former mentor, he burst into tears. "Samuel's dead, Mr. Dwight! He died two weeks ago, and from the time he got Science's remedy until he went to see Jesus, he screamed about his chest hurting! I had to watch him suffer until . . ." Reggie trailed off and wiped his eyes with his paw. "My birthday is tomorrow and then I'll be old enough for the drug. I don't want to die! Will you hide me?"

Dwight's face fell. "Of course, son."

But Reggie wasn't the only youth wanting help. Soon, a half dozen baby gators showed up, babies with their birthdays and the remedy looming. Night after night Dwight took them in, because baby gators were just that, baby gators, not animals to be laid on the altar of a society's fear.

Now, one would think that the gator parents would get suspicious of where their young had gone, and to some extent they did. However, they were all too preoccupied by Science's remedy and making sure every gator in Gator Glade had it to chase them down. In addition, no one wanted to go near Dwight on account of his being unclean by not taking the remedy. It was then that Dwight counted his apartheid as a blessing.

The sad thing in all of this was that despite the jabs, weak hearts, broken families, and missing young'uns, the fish still came.

The fish still attacked.

And the fish still ate—more frequently and boldly than ever before, terrorizing Gator Glade so much that the screams from the adult gators rang out through the humid Florida nights. One night, it got so bad that the gators were driven to within a foot of Dwight's end of the bank, the moonlight bathing a struggle in the bayou.

Then, Dwight could take no more. He put Reggie in charge of the young'uns. "If I don't come back, take the others north. Follow the Florida Man trail 'cross the banks until you run into a ramshackle shed and a gator named Jethro what lives with a human named Jeremiah. You tell him you know me, and he'll take ya'll in."

"What are you gonna do, Mr. Dwight?"

"I'm gonna eat the fish!"

"But Mr. Dwight—they're mutant fish!"

Dwight looked at Reggie. "They's still fish, and I'm still a gator, dagnabbit! God made gators to eat fish, and that's what I'm gonna do!"

Then Dwight was off like a shot through the water, nose aimed at the bloody waves. Mayor Crassy was crying amidst them, his scaly arms flailing as though he had forgotten how to swim. Dwight forced his large body in and thrashed his tail to corral the menace away from the politician. Then he snapped down hard, filling his mouth with the teeming menace. They tasted fizzy, like a soda can he'd bit down on once, but by no means bad or unnatural.

"There, Dwight, over there!" Mayor Crassy was pointing to a churning deluge. This time Gerald was in trouble. Dwight veered over, snapping and chomping until those fish were gone, too. A grateful Gerald looked at him. "Dwight," he said, "I'm sorry, I'm so . . ."

But before Gerald could finish, another churning surfaced. Dwight pushed Gerald aside and opened his jaws once more. He swallowed four, five, six times until his belly was full and he felt ready to vomit. Still the waters teamed, and just when he felt he could eat no more, a familiar whooping voice rang out:

"Whoooeehhhh! That's some appetite you got there, boy! How's about saving some for me and my Florida Man? I tell you what—he loves them pee-ranas!"

"Jethro?" Dwight exclaimed hopefully, and sure enough his cousin surfaced, flashing a set of crooked teeth! He winked at Dwight, then started corralling the murderous fish while a purring sound emerged from the night, along with a modest fishing boat piloted by Jethro's skinny human, Jeremiah.

Jeremiah muttered something half Cajun, half English, and all Florida Man as he tossed out a large net on one side and bags of marshmallows on the other.

The gators ate a few of the treats, but Dwight was too full to enjoy. Instead, he watched, glassy eyed and grateful as Jethro drove the remaining fish into Jeremiah's net and then used his large body to help lift them onto the boat. A minute later, the waters were calm—full of only moonlight and marshmallows.

The baby gators, who until that moment had been hiding on the shoreline, let out several squeals of joy and ambled into the water to consume the fluffy desserts. Meanwhile, Reggie headed straight for his dad. They looked at each other for a moment, the sorrow in Reggie's eyes matching the regret in Gerald's. Then, the two embraced. The rules of the apartheid were forgotten between them.

"You mean, all this time, you and your Florida Man have been eating these mutated fish?" Mayor Crassy asked Jethro. He seemed very humbled.

"*Mutated?*" Jethro laughed heartily. "These fish ain't mutated! They's pee-ranas! You know, exotic type pets. Like me!" Jethro batted his eyes. "But the human what had them blew hisself up, so now they's lunch. And they is gooood! Matter of fact, we came down here 'specially to find 'em since our end of the swamp run out."

Jeremiah laughed and mumbled something unintelligible to all but Jethro.

"You're right, Jeremiah. We best be getting these to our smoke pit!" Jethro leaned over to Mayor Crassy. "Not to brag, but my Jeremiah is one top-notch chef! I can't wait to see what he does tonight!"

Jeremiah let out an appreciative chuckle and slapped the side of his vessel as a warning to the gators before starting up his motor and angling it back the way he had come.

"Well, thanks for sharin', ya'll! You know, Dwight," Jethro looked at his cousin, "I ain't seen ya in a dog's age. Bring yourself up to my place sometime. I'll have Jeremiah make you something real fine!"

"I'll do that, Jethro," Dwight said, waving goodbye. Soon, Jethro and Jeremiah faded into the night.

Beside Dwight, an apologetic Gerald and Mayor Crassy floated in the water. Now that the swamp had calmed, Dwight suddenly realized that they were the only adult gators present. "Where's Science? And Merv? And Marjorie?" Dwight asked.

"They all fell prey to the fish two nights ago," Mayor Crassy noted sadly.

"As did my wife," Gerald mourned, pulling Reggie in to comfort him. It was the first little Reggie heard of his mother's death, and naturally the little gator started sobbing.

"Dwight, we owe you an apology," said Mayor Crassy.

"That we do," Gerald added sadly. "We were so caught up in staying alive, we didn't realize we weren't living. Worse, we were losing ourselves and our loved ones to something far worse than the fish: to the apartheid of the swamp."

Lightning Source UK Ltd.
Milton Keynes UK
UKHW020631031222
413194UK00018B/1076